"You've Called Me Callie All Evening,"

she murmured, looking thoughtful. "Why? Is your not calling me by my last name part of your effort to work things out professionally?"

"I don't always call you by your last name."

"You did until today."

Trey flinched. When had she become "Callie" and not "Sheely" to him?

A good question. Callie appeared only in his steamy, erotic dreams, while dependable, sexless Sheely remained the perfect helpmate in the OR.

But at some point—he couldn't exactly pinpoint when—the sexy nighttime dream girl and his faithful daytime partner had fused into one and the same woman. A woman he admired and relied upon.

A woman he wanted.

Dear Reader,

This Fourth of July, join in the fireworks of Silhouette's 20th anniversary year by reading all six powerful, passionate, provocative love stories from Silhouette Desire!

July's MAN OF THE MONTH is a *Bachelor Doctor* by Barbara Boswell. Sparks ignite when a dedicated doctor discovers his passion for his loyal nurse!

With *Midnight Fantasy,* beloved author Ann Major launches an exciting new promotion in Desire called BODY & SOUL. Our BODY & SOUL books are among the most sensuous and emotionally intense you'll ever read. Every woman wants to be loved…BODY & SOUL, and in these books you'll find a heady combination of breathtaking love and tumultuous desire.

Amy J. Fetzer continues her popular WIFE, INC. miniseries with *Wife for Hire.* Enjoy *Ride a Wild Heart,* the first sexy installment of Peggy Moreland's miniseries TEXAS GROOMS. This month, Desire offers you a terrific two-books-in-one value—*Blood Brothers* by Anne McAllister and Lucy Gordon. A British lord and an American cowboy are look-alike cousins who switch lives temporarily…and lose their hearts for good in this romance equivalent of a doubleheader. And don't miss the debut of Kristi Gold, with her moving love story *Cowboy for Keeps*—it's a keeper!

So make your summer sizzle—treat yourself to all six of these sultry Desire romances!

Happy Reading!

Joan Marlow Golan

Joan Marlow Golan
Senior Editor, Silhouette Desire

Please address questions and book requests to:
Silhouette Reader Service
U.S.: 3010 Walden Ave., P.O. Box 1325, Buffalo, NY 14269
Canadian: P.O. Box 609, Fort Erie, Ont. L2A 5X3

Bachelor Doctor
BARBARA BOSWELL

Silhouette®

Desire

Published by Silhouette Books

America's Publisher of Contemporary Romance

SILHOUETTE BOOKS

ISBN 0-373-76303-4

BACHELOR DOCTOR

This edition published by arrangement with Harlequin Books S.A.

® and TM are trademarks of Harlequin Books S.A., used under license. Trademarks indicated with ® are registered in the United States Patent and Trademark Office, the Canadian Trade Marks Office and in other countries.

Visit Silhouette at www.eHarlequin.com

Printed in U.S.A.

Books by Barbara Boswell

Silhouette Desire

Rule Breaker #558
Another Whirlwind Courtship #583
The Bridal Price #609
The Baby Track #651
License To Love #685
Double Trouble #749
Triple Treat #787
The Best Revenge #821
Family Feud #877
*The Engagement Party #932
The Wilde Bunch #943
Who's the Boss? #1069
The Brennan Baby #1123
That Marriageable Man! #1147
Forever Flint #1243
Bachelor Doctor #1303

*Always a Bridesmaid!

Silhouette Books

Fortune's Children
Stand-In Bride

A Fortune's Children Wedding:
  The Hoodwinked Bride

BARBARA BOSWELL

loves writing about families. "I guess family has been a big influence on my writing," she says. "I particularly enjoy writing about how my characters' family relationships affect them."

When Barbara isn't writing and reading, she's spending time with her *own* family—her husband, three daughters and three cats, whom she concedes are the true bosses of their home! She has lived in Europe, but now makes her home in Pennsylvania. She collects miniatures and holiday ornaments, tries to avoid exercise and has somehow found the time to write over twenty category romances.

IT'S OUR 20th ANNIVERSARY!
We'll be celebrating all year,
Continuing with these fabulous titles,
On sale in July 2000.

Intimate Moments

#1015 Egan Cassidy's Kid
Beverly Barton

#1016 Mission: Irresistible
Sharon Sala

#1017 The Once and Future Father
Marie Ferrarella

#1018 Imminent Danger
Carla Cassidy

#1019 The Detective's Undoing
Jill Shalvis

#1020 Who's Been Sleeping in Her Bed?
Pamela Dalton

Special Edition

#1333 The Pint-Sized Secret
Sherryl Woods

#1334 Man of Passion
Lindsay McKenna

#1335 Whose Baby Is This?
Patricia Thayer

#1336 Married to a Stranger
Allison Leigh

#1337 Doctor and the Debutante
Pat Warren

#1338 Maternal Instincts
Beth Henderson

Desire

#1303 Bachelor Doctor
Barbara Boswell

#1304 Midnight Fantasy
Ann Major

#1305 Wife for Hire
Amy J. Fetzer

#1306 Ride a Wild Heart
Peggy Moreland

#1307 Blood Brothers
Anne McAllister & Lucy Gordon

#1308 Cowboy for Keeps
Kristi Gold

Romance

#1456 Falling for Grace
Stella Bagwell

#1457 The Borrowed Groom
Judy Christenberry

#1458 Denim & Diamond
Moyra Tarling

#1459 The Monarch's Son
Valerie Parv

#1460 Jodie's Mail-Order Man
Julianna Morris

#1461 Lassoed!
Martha Shields

One

Operating room one was crowded with observers watching Dr. Trey Weldon, neurosurgeon extraordinaire, at work. The patient's condition had been deemed hopeless until his referral to Dr. Weldon, who had offered a ray of hope in a daring yet promising experimental procedure developed by the gifted surgeon himself.

"It's mobbed in here today," a wide-eyed medical student murmured to no one in particular. "This is the hottest show in the entire med center. Everybody wants to observe the master at work."

"Yeah. Dr. Weldon rules!" enthused another awestruck med student.

"Quiet!" A nursing student reprimanded the pair. "Dr. Weldon is speaking." The name was said with hushed reverence.

Dr. Trey Weldon, in the midst of explaining the intricacies of AVMs or arteriovenous malformations—tangled or malformed arteries or veins in the brain that over time became dilated, exerting pressure or bursting—overheard the students and automatically lifted his eyes to meet the eyes of his chief scrub nurse, Callie Sheely.

Their gazes connected for only a fraction of a second, but it was long enough for Trey to see a flash of humor light those big dark eyes of hers. He knew she had overheard the students, too, knew that she was smiling beneath her surgical mask.

His lips twisted into a smile behind his own mask. He'd known Callie would find the students' overexaggerated hype as amusing as he did.

There had been a time, not very long ago, when he wouldn't have seen the humor in such remarks. Of course, he wouldn't have considered the students' adulation to be overexaggerated hype, either. Over the years he had grown so accustomed to lavish praise that he simply accepted it as a given.

Until Callie Sheely. From her he'd come to view certain things—like extravagant compliments—from a different angle. Trey thought back to that fateful time he'd spied Callie grinning in the background while some junior colleagues expressed their excessive admiration of him, to him.

When he asked her about it later, she'd snickered, unrepentant. It amused her to hear people fawn over him, she'd said. Listening to his minions try to outdo each other while shoveling the…praise, invariably gave her a hearty chuckle.

Minions? Shoveling? Trey well remembered his own astonishment at her frankness. No one had ever made such a remark to him before, and only Callie Sheely continued to make similar impertinent jests about him, to him.

But instead of being irked—Trey admittedly didn't tolerate frivolity or nonsense very well—he had found himself seeing the humor. Sharing her amusement.

"Of course, they genuinely do admire you," she'd also assured him, and Trey had found *himself* snickering, a rare event in itself. As a rule he did not snicker.

However, Callie's warm assertion had touched a humorous, previously unstruck, chord within him. As if he cared whether he was admired by junior toadies, as if he needed anyone's assurance about anything! The very idea was laughable.

And now whenever anyone laid on the compliments or the hero worship a tad too thick, he looked at Callie, and they would share a silent, mutual moment of mirth.

Trey continued performing the operation, explaining the procedure to his audience while he worked, all the while contemplating Callie Sheely's irreverence toward his lordly reputation.

He had been blessed with the ability to think and do several different things simultaneously, while keeping each separate and exact. It was a gift he took for granted, having always possessed it.

He flicked his finger slightly, and Callie immediately handed him what he wanted, a small sharp scalpel, an instrument he'd redesigned and then had reduced to near doll-size for certain specific uses, today's operation being one of them.

He rarely had to ask Callie for instruments during an operation, not unless an unforeseen complication occurred and he had to improvise on the spot.

Otherwise, she routinely remembered which one was used for what from previous operations, and when he was going to try something new, he would go over the procedure with her beforehand, taking her through it step by step. She filed away what he told her in her head, using the information to expertly assist him.

Trey admired her excellent memory and OR nursing skills as much as he did her unruffled calm under pressure. He had never worked so well with anyone before, never been so in sync with another person as he was with Callie Sheely during surgery. While in the OR, it was as if she were an extension of himself.

It was new to him, this kind of intuitive rapport. Certainly it had never existed in his personal life and still didn't. Yet here in the OR he and Callie were as one, working together in uncommon unity and intimacy.

He lifted his gaze to meet Callie's again. She had the most beautiful, expressive eyes he'd ever seen, a dark liquid velvet glowing with warmth and intelligence, alert with liveliness and—

"Any questions?" Trey deliberately interrupted his own reverie.

Lately, renegade thoughts about Callie Sheely seemed to strike him more and more frequently. Whether in the OR or alone in his apartment or chatting with colleagues anytime, anywhere, random images of Callie Sheely would suddenly pop into his head. He would find himself drifting off on a mental riff, mulling over her memory, her eyes, her humor.

Such thoughts had no place in a professional relationship, Trey reminded himself. And a professional relationship was the only type he and Callie Sheely had. The only kind of relationship they would ever have, and that was the way he wanted it, the way it had to be.

Still, his unexpected musings were beginning to bother him. After all, Trey Weldon's finely honed mind did *not* drift into unfitting flights of fancy.

Except lately, when it did. And inevitably the disconcerting drift was Callie Sheely inspired.

"I repeat, any questions?" He heard the impatient edge in his tone.

Well, he *was* impatient, though not really with the students who remained silent, perhaps intimidated.

"So I can assume that everybody perfectly understands everything there is to know about AVMs and this procedure?" It was a short step from impatience to sarcasm, and Trey couldn't resist taking it.

At last one of the med students dutifully piped up with a question. True, it was a stupid question, but then the kid was merely a student. Trey took pity on him and proceeded to answer in painstaking detail.

He determinedly put aside any more thoughts about Callie Sheely's eyes. He refused to think about her marvelous memory or her invaluable OR skills, either. He particularly refused to ponder their intuitive rapport and the way her sense of humor had somehow infected him.

She was not getting under his skin, Trey assured himself.

They were colleagues. They worked together, nothing more. They weren't even friends, because friends socialized outside the workplace, and he and Callie Sheely never saw each other except in the workplace.

And that was the way he liked it, the way he wanted it to be.

No, she was *not* getting under his skin.

Chief OR scrub nurse Callie Sheely listened to every word of Trey Weldon's comprehensive explanation. As always the mellifluous timbre of his voice stirred her. Only Trey could sound seductive while discussing the complexities of AVMs and their variations, along with inventive ways to repair them.

Callie watched him work, anticipating what he would do next and what surgical instrument he would need, his voice keeping her focused even as it enthralled her. Excited her. Trey Weldon had the sexiest voice she'd ever heard, deep and masculine, mesmerizing, with just the slightest hint of an upper-class Virginia drawl.

If only he sounded like Elmer Fudd, she lamented wistfully. As a diversion Callie tried to imagine Elmer pronouncing arteriovenous. She had to do *something* to decrease the sensual effect Trey's voice had on her.

It just wasn't fair! Not only was her boss good-looking, brilliant and talented, but he had a voice that could net him a fortune doing romance-hero readings for books on tape. And she had to listen to it, to him, by the hour and was expected to remain completely immune to him and his powerful allure.

After all, Callie knew the rules. She was Trey's coworker, his subordinate, actually, and she knew that was the only way Trey Weldon saw her. Would ever see her.

She viewed their situation as comparable to characters in the old Greek myths, which she'd enjoyed reading as a child on her biweekly trips to the Carnegie library. In those myths, gods who dwelt high in Mount Olympus did not consort with ordinary mortals. Just as upper-class scions like Trey Weldon didn't socialize with working-class nurses from Pittsburgh. Like Callie Sheely.

Ancient and fanciful they might be, but those myths taught a necessary counterlesson to the fairy tales that Callie had also devoured as a child. In fairy tales, a scullery maid might land a prince, but not in real life.

Real life meant sticking with your own kind. Otherwise the result was culture clash, not romance.

Callie suppressed a sigh, wishing that Trey would lapse into silence so the music could be cranked up to full volume. The OR team took turns choosing what was to be played, and today's choice had been Quiana Turner's, the circulating nurse. That meant sassy girl singers, lively and loud and brimming with attitude, just what Callie needed to hear.

But Trey continued to explain what he was doing to the students, and Callie listened and watched as he skillfully wielded the tiny scalpel she'd handed him.

His technique was flawless. As always she was awed by his incredible dexterity, his seemingly effortless expertise. To use such a tiny instrument so effectively in one of the most crucial parts of the brain was true genius. She never tired of watching him perform.

Nobody else did, either. To say that Dr. Trey Weldon, Tri-State Medical Center's extraordinarily gifted neurosurgeon, was respected by his peers, by his lesser colleagues, by the establishment powers that be and everybody else, was a pallid understatement.

Trey Weldon was a star, a "surgical supernova" to quote a dazzled science reporter from the local Pittsburgh newspaper. The article exalted Trey's operating prowess and his impressive credentials, also mentioning the determination of the medical center's administrators to recruit him eighteen months ago.

Callie had saved that article and read it from time to time, particularly when she felt herself in danger of forgetting just how far she was—and would always be—from Trey Weldon's world. Beginning, appropriately enough, with their origins.

The Weldon family descended from landed gentry in colonial Virginia, whose fortune had been made generations ago while Callie's forebears were still trying to eke out a living as peasants in the old country. And though different backgrounds often didn't matter, Callie knew bloodlines meant a lot to the aristocratic Weldon family.

It would certainly matter to them that her blood was the wrong shade of blue—that is, blue-collar blue. She just knew it would, from what she'd gleaned from that newspaper article and some of the casual comments made by Trey himself.

The son of Winston and Laura Weldon—she'd learned his parents' names from the article, too—had nothing socially in common with her, the daughter of Jack and Nancy Sheely, whose grandparents had left poverty in Ireland and Russia to live in poverty in Pittsburgh. Their brave move and hard work had eventually paid off for their children and grandchildren, but high society they weren't.

The Weldons were and had been Southern aristocracy for a couple of centuries.

"Holding up okay?" Trey's inquiry nearly startled Callie into dropping a gauze sponge. Thankfully, her reflexes were too sharp to permit such a lapse.

"Me?" she murmured, trying to suppress her astonishment.

Trey had ceased lecturing and was asking her a personal question. If she was holding up okay. That had never happened before.

She'd been with him in surgery for nine or ten hours straight without him once mentioning thirst, hunger, sore muscles—or even the need for a bathroom break. He didn't acknowledge such mundane concerns, for himself or others.

"Sheely?" he prompted, and his brow furrowed with what might have been concern.

"I'm fine," she said quickly. But she was perplexed by his unusual solicitousness. Did she look ready to drop or something? Or to drop something? He wouldn't like that!

"Honest," she added quickly.

Trey nodded his head and went on operating.

While others withered around him, Trey Weldon just kept on going.

"To watch Trey Weldon operate on a brain is to experience a virtuoso at the top of his game," Jimmy Dimarino, a first-year general surgery resident—and on some days an aspiring neurosurgeon himself—often enthused to Callie.

Jimmy tried to attend as many of Dr. Weldon's operations as he could, badgering Callie for scheduling information. As the chief scrub nurse on Trey Weldon's handpicked OR team for the past twelve months, Callie knew what procedure was slated and when; she was also privy to the emergency schedule.

She shared the inside scoop with Jimmy because they went way back, to the bad old days of elementary school when they'd lived next door to each other. Somehow their relationship had survived a brief eighth-grade romance, too. These days, Jimmy's long-term fondness for Callie had been elevated to outright admiration—due in large part to her access to Dr. Trey Weldon.

"The AVM has been repaired," Trey announced. "We

were able to avoid any undue disturbance of the surrounding brain tissue, so the patient's recovery ought to be swift and unremarkable."

He made it sound like a decree that would naturally be obeyed. Callie smiled behind her surgical mask, then lifted her eyes to see Trey looking directly at her.

For one seemingly endless moment, time stood still as their gazes met and held.

And then: "Fritche, close," Trey ordered with a nod toward one of the residents. He moved away from the table amidst murmurs of praise and appreciation, even a smattering of applause.

Scott Fritche, a first-year neurosurgical resident, stepped up to close, a task often given to underlings to further their experience.

Callie stayed where she was, assisting Scott Fritche, handing him the necessary instruments, sponges and sutures, subtly guiding him, before he needed to ask for anything.

She'd worked with Fritche a few times before, during his general-surgery residency, preceding this one, before she had become a permanent member of Trey's team. But she didn't remember Fritche being quite as ham-handed as he was today.

"I swear it took Fritche longer to close than for Trey to perform the entire operation," complained Quiana Turner, as she and Callie trooped out of the OR, tugging off their masks.

Callie smiled at Quiana's exaggeration. "We've gotten spoiled, working with Trey," she conceded. "He's a tough act for anybody to follow, let alone a resident."

"Fritche sure isn't the hotshot he thinks he is," Leo Arkis said, sneering.

Leo did the advance OR work for the Weldon team and also served as backup relief to Callie or Quiana when necessary. "Could that clod have done any worse in there, messing up sutures and dropping sponges like a flower girl tossing rose petals at a wedding?''

"That's kind of harsh, Leo. Fritche wasn't all *that* bad," chided Callie. "He's inexperienced and he was nervous but—"

"I wish we'd called Trey back in to watch that jerk at work," Leo cut in. "It would've been a kick seeing the icy wrath of our boss freeze Fritche into a human Popsicle."

Callie arched her dark brows. "Leo, I know how you feel about Fritche, but ratting on him to Trey is—"

She broke off in midsentence because Dr. Trey Weldon stood in the middle of the newly renovated lounge, which the trio had just entered.

He was pulling his scrub shirt over his head.

The sight of him stopped Callie in her tracks, rendering her speechless. Trey tossed the shirt aside and stood barechested, the strong, well-defined muscles of his chest and shoulders revealed in the fluorescent glow of the overhead lights. His green scrub pants rode low on his waist, displaying the flat belly, a deep-set navel and a sprinkling of dark, wiry hair arrowing downward.

In the year that she'd been working on his team, Callie had seen Trey Weldon in scrubs too many times to count. But she hadn't seen what lay beneath them. Until this moment.

Her mouth was suddenly quite dry.

"God bless this new unisex lounge," murmured Quiana, staring appreciatively at Trey. "Next, I hope they combine the locker rooms."

"Ratting on who?" Trey asked, his eyes on Callie. "What are you talking about, Sheely?"

It seemed that he had overheard at least part of what she'd said.

Callie's dark eyes widened, and she forced herself to concentrate. She knew Trey wouldn't like what they'd been talking about, and she wasn't eager to be the one to tell him about Fritche's less-than-stellar-performance. Errors, in general, annoyed Trey, but an error in his operating room... *yikes!*

Trey Weldon didn't make mistakes in the operating room, had not even come close to one during the entire year that Callie had been working with him. No, this wasn't a conversation she cared to continue with him.

"Ever hear the old saying of All's Well That Ends Well?" she asked hopefully. "Let's just say it applies in this case."

It was an optimistic approach, she knew. Trey had no patience with those who wasted his time by not supplying him with the answers he wanted. He was looking impatient now. Impatient—and shirtless and muscular.

"Sheely," Trey was already verging on testy. He directed a blue-eyed laser stare at her. "Stop talking in riddles."

Callie flicked the tip of her tongue nervously over her top lip. Why did he have to grill her while standing there, half-nude? The sight was wreaking havoc with her thought processes. "Well, uh—"

"I don't know if you'd call this ratting, Trey," Leo spoke up. "But Fritche screwed up in there today. I thought you ought to know," he added righteously.

Trey's face went dark as a sky before a tornado was about to strike. "Is my patient—"

"He's fine," Callie said quickly. "Fritche made a few mistakes, correctable ones. The patient is fine," she affirmed. "We would've called you the second anything turned bad."

"That's not good enough," Trey snapped. "I expect to be called the second *before* anything turns bad."

"Luckily it didn't even get that far because Sheely was right there before No-Opposable-Thumbs Fritche could do any damage," Leo hastened to assure him. "Honest, there was no harm done, Trey."

"Okay, then." Trey gave Leo a fraternal slap on the

shoulder. "I can always count on you to be frank and up-front with me, can't I, Leo?" His slight smile instantly faded when he turned back to Callie. "What about you, Sheely?" Trey's expression darkened further. "I want a word with you, Sheely. Now."

His big hand cupped her elbow, and he walked her a few feet away, turning her aside, his six-foot frame blocking her view of the other two.

His hand stayed on her elbow, and Callie tried hard not to notice. Trey frequently touched her, placing his hand on the small of her back or on her shoulder when she preceded him through doors, curling his fingers around her wrist while enthusiastically describing something neurosurgical, cupping her elbow to guide her wherever.

She pretended to pay no attention to his touch because she knew Trey himself was oblivious to it, as oblivious as he was to her as an individual. As a woman. His touch was automatic and unaware, definitely nothing personal. He would clasp her wrist as one might grip a pencil, she knew that his hand on her back or her elbow was akin to him resting his palm on a railing.

There were times when she wished she actually were the inanimate object Trey Weldon considered her to be. It would be so much easier—on her nerves, on her senses. The warm strength of his fingers on her skin evoked sensations that were hopelessly, girlishly romantic. And embarrassing because it was all so futile.

Sometimes, alone in bed in the darkness of her room at night, Callie pondered the irony of the situation. That she—who had always been so sensible and practical, who'd never suffered any hopeless, girlish, embarrassing yearnings, not even as an adolescent, when almost everybody else did—would be struck with this acute *crush* at the mature age of twenty-six.

The situation appalled her. She had a crush on her boss! Worse, she was a nurse with a crush on a doctor. Might as well throw in their class differences too; the proletarian yearning for the lord of the manor. A triple cliché, and she was living it. What unparalleled humiliation! Especially since her crush was entirely unrequited.

Callie refused to kid herself, to even pretend that Trey gave her a thought outside the operating room. Of course he didn't. And though she continually fought her feelings for him, his touch and his penetrating stare affected her viscerally.

There didn't seem to be anything she could do about that, but she could keep it her most-closely guarded secret. Which she had, quite successfully.

No one, especially not Trey, ever had to know about the sweet, syrupy warmth that flowed through her at his slightest touch. Nor would she ever reveal the sharp ache that sometimes threatened to bring her to her knees when his deep-blue eyes looked into hers.

Except right now those blue eyes of his were hard and cold with anger. If any stare could freeze a hapless recipient into a human Popsicle, it would be the one Trey was directing at her at this moment.

Callie met and held his eyes, a sheer act of will on her part. And not at all easy because Trey Weldon had perfected—or maybe he'd naturally been gifted with—the art of nonverbal intimidation. Not that he was a slouch in the verbal intimidation department, either.

But Callie never crumbled or froze in response to Trey's ire, verbal or non. Because she knew that Trey expected her to be as tough and unemotional as he was himself? Because she knew he *needed* her to be that way?

Callie nearly groaned aloud. She was doing it again, seeking evidence that Trey Weldon thought of her as something more than merely a set of rubber-gloved hands assisting him in the OR.

"I expect better from you, Sheely." Trey glared at her in

the coldly unnerving way that had reduced other recipients to tears.

But not Callie. She had once overheard him tell Leo, "Sheely is tough. She's the only woman I've ever worked with who's never cried. Not a tear, not once."

It was untrue, of course, further proof of how little he knew about her. She'd wept over their saddest cases, her heart breaking for the devastated families of patients unable to be saved, even by Trey Weldon's formidable skills.

But she'd never cried in front of Trey Weldon, not a tear, not once. Callie knew Trey's remark to Leo was a high compliment indeed, and she intended to keep her record of tearlessness in his company intact.

"The patients deserve better from you, Sheely," snarled Trey. "They deserve your best, and when you put anything else ahead of—"

"I put nothing ahead of our patients' well-being. They get the best that I have to give, *Dr. Weldon*." Callie tried to match his cold tones but couldn't. His particular way of expressing anger through iciness was unique to him.

Which didn't mean she couldn't communicate her own anger in her own way. Nothing, *nothing* infuriated her more than to have her commitment to her patients and to her job disparaged. To have her professionalism questioned.

And for Trey Weldon to do so…when she'd worked so hard for him, *for their patients*… Callie let her own fury displace the hurt that sliced through her, deep and sharp.

Her voice rose, and her dark eyes blazed, her rage as hot as his was cold. "And as for Scott Fritche, he was simply nervous today, *Dr. Weldon*. Fritche is in his first year of neurosurgery, he is inexperienced and he was suddenly expected to perform in front of an audience of—"

"Stop making excuses for him, Sheely!" Trey cut in. He held her glare. "It's unacceptable."

Neither bothered to blink. Or to move. They stood locked in their own world, anything and everyone else excluded.

Callie pulled off her surgical cap and threw it into a tall laundry bin. Her ponytail, which had been stuffed inside the cap, tumbled free, the ends swiping the nape of her neck.

If you lose your temper, you lose. One of her dad's adages popped into Callie's head. Too late. She'd gone ahead and lost her temper, anyway. Now she might as well go for broke.

"Unacceptable?" she huffed. "So are you going to fire me?" It was a dare, a challenge. Callie held her breath.

"Here we go again!" Leo heaved a dramatic groan. He and Quiana had moved closer, the better to listen to every word that passed between Trey and Callie. "It's like seeing a rerun on TV for the four hundredth time—you know every word of the dialogue. C'mon Quiana, let's get some lunch."

"Might as well," agreed Quiana.

The two exited the lounge, heading for the cafeteria.

"The four hundredth time?" Trey looked bewildered.

"Not even close," murmured Callie, a pale pink flush staining her cheeks.

Okay, she hadn't gone for broke, she silently conceded. When she felt Trey was being insufferably imperious, she would respond by getting mad and inviting him to fire her.

The first time, it had just slipped out, and she'd waited in agony, expecting him to fire her outright. But he hadn't, and then she'd said it again—and again and again—and by now she pretty much knew Trey wouldn't fire her. Was absolutely sure of it, in fact.

But she hadn't said it four hundred times!

"No, I am not going to fire you, but—" Trey broke off, suddenly looking almost comically astonished. "So *that's* what Leo meant when he was talking about seeing a rerun for the four hundredth time and knowing the dialogue. He was talking about that 'going to fire me?' habit of yours."

"Duh," Callie muttered darkly. Trey would *have* to pick right now to finally decipher one of Leo's stupid jokes. "And it's not a *habit.* Leo overexaggerates."

"Not this time, he didn't. It's true. You practically dare me to fire you, Sheely. Did it ever occur to you that sometime I might say yes and just go ahead and do it?"

"Oh, maybe the first three hundred times." Callie was sarcastic. "But the last hundred times or so, I felt my job was safe enough."

Trey's dark brows narrowed. "Nobody talks to me the way you do, Sheely."

"Is that a threat?" Callie squared her shoulders and lifted her head, trying to make herself as tall and formidable as possible. Unfortunately her five-foot, four-inch frame remained dwarfed by Trey.

"Don't go nuclear, Sheely, it wasn't a threat. It was simply a statement of fact. Nobody around here talks to me the way you do."

"Well, no wonder." She folded her arms in front of her chest in classic defensive position. Just because she had a crush on him didn't mean she would permit herself to be crushed by him.

"You're practically a god around here. Nobody can believe you actually *chose* to come to Pittsburgh when you could've gone to any hospital in the country. Needless to say, without exception, people speak reverently to you."

"It seems that Leo isn't the only one on this team who overexaggerates." Trey looked irked. "And maybe you can explain why Pittsburghers are forever apologizing for the city. Why do they feel the need to put it down, especially if a nonnative says something complimentary about the place? Which brings us to, Why wouldn't I actually *choose* to come here, Sheely?"

"Why would you choose Pittsburgh's Tri-State Medical Center when you could've gone to Johns Hopkins or Mass General or Duke or places equally prestigious? Is that a rhetorical question or am I supposed to answer it?"

"You see, you just did it again!" Trey exclaimed. "Another putdown of your hometown. What's with you Pittsburghers?"

"We don't like bragging, so we don't embellish. We simply state the facts—which is what I was doing," retorted Callie. "You went to medical school at Duke and did your surgical residency at Johns Hopkins, then on to Mass General for your neurosurgery residency and fellowship. You could write your own ticket anywhere. Why would you come to—"

"Don't forget to mention my exclusive New England prep school and my undergraduate bioengineering degree from MIT, Sheely."

"Which enables you to custom design the surgical instruments that you—" Callie broke off and stared at him. "You were being ironically droll."

"And that makes you gape?"

"*More* drollery?"

"Ah, your jaw drops even farther."

"All right, I admit I'm stunned. For your to joke about your hallowed credentials is something like hearing a saint wisecracking about divinity."

"Sheely," he paused and frowned. "Don't put me on a pedestal." She had the usual misconception about the blueness of his blood, Trey realized, and her next words confirmed it.

"I don't have to, you're already up there. I expect you were born there—and you're well aware of it, too."

A man like Trey Weldon, brilliant, handsome, successful—a man like that, who had it all, had to be aware of his status, his desirability. And not only neurosurgically speaking. He was one of the most eligible bachelors in the city—in the entire state of Pennsylvania, not to mention his own native state of Virginia!

Callie herself had seen how women here at the hospital practically threw themselves at his feet. She and Leo and Quiana enjoyed countless jokes about that. At least, Leo and

Quiana enjoyed the jokes. Callie's laughter rang hollow in her own ears. Worse, she could only imagine how very sought-after Trey was in exalted social circles, far removed from the hospital grounds.

She took another long look at his bare chest, and fury abruptly flared within her. "And we aren't in a...a gym!" she snapped. "Put on your shirt. Please," she added, because, after all, she was talking to her boss.

Trey picked up the scrub shirt he'd dropped onto a chair and pulled it over his head, inside out. "I'm not following." He gave an exasperated huff. "What on earth are we talking about now, Sheely?"

Scowling, he ran his hand over his brown hair, a dark-chestnut shade, always cut short for practical and hygenic reasons.

Callie caught herself wondering if his hair felt as thick and springy as it looked. It took a moment for her to remember what they'd been talking about. "We're discussing your beyond-impeccable credentials," she said edgily.

Trey gave a wave of his hand, visibly impatient. "Let's get back to the real subject at hand, Sheely."

Callie proceeded to describe in detail each of Scott Fritche's minor but time-consuming mistakes. "It's not an enormous deal, Trey, though Leo's done his best to make you think it is. We've both watched other residents, with more experience than Scott Fritche, do far worse with no unfavorable results. So you see—"

"What I see is that Arkis and Turner were right. You really did save Fritche's ass in there, Sheely. Not to mention our poor patient's cranium." Trey folded his arms in front of his chest, but the gesture wasn't a defensive one for him.

Oh, yes, he was infinitely gifted in the body language of intimidation. However, Callie wasn't intimidated. Instead, observing the way his muscles rippled when he moved his arms, studying the breadth of his shoulders, she was... aroused.

She was practically ogling him! Callie caught herself and quickly averted her gaze, fixing it on the poster tacked up on the wall beyond him.

It was an advertisement for the Hospital Auxiliary's Annual Springtime Ball, a popular fund-raiser held in early April, when the region's weather was still more like winter than spring, despite the calendar.

Unlike those charity balls sponsored by exclusive women's clubs, where the price of admission was astronomically high, thus limiting the guests to the social elite, the Tri-State Hospital's auxiliary set aside a large block of tickets at lower prices, affordable to the hospital staff.

Everybody from student nurses to interns and residents, from the hospital administrators and lordly attending physicians to various corporate benefactors, politicos and the local pillars of society, attended the Springtime Ball. Somehow, the eclectic mix worked. Each year the ball topped the previous one's record for ticket sales and attendance.

Callie had gone every year since nursing school. Often with Jimmy, sometimes with other escorts, always friends. This year she'd made no plans to attend. She couldn't seem to work up any enthusiasm for going.

Her eyes darted to Trey. He was glaring at her.

"Sheely, if it isn't too much trouble, could you stop drifting off and at least make a pretense of staying on topic? That would be Scott Fritche who endangered my patient in the OR. Remember?"

Callie's eyes, dark as onyx, grew round as saucers. "The patient wasn't endangered, honestly." She caught her lower lip between her teeth and took a deep breath. "I was right there, Trey, I knew what to do. Of course, I would've called for you the second *before* anything could have gone wrong."

Trey straightened, looking even taller to her. "You know I expect my team to be like cogs in a perfectly run machine,

Sheely. We simply can't afford any mistakes and we can't succumb to—''

"I know. And woe to the cog that slips, even slightly. Leo and Quiana and I—''

"This isn't about you three, I know how good you are. You're the best in the area. I watched you for six months before handpicking you myself for my team. But Fritche is another story entirely. If he's no good, we've got to get him out of the neurosurgery program sooner rather than later, before he does irreparable harm.''

"Trey, before we go any further with this, maybe you should know that Leo holds a personal grudge against Scott Fritche. I don't think I'd be exaggerating to say that if Leo could hurt Scott, he would. Oh, not physically. But he'd certainly settle for doing damage to Scott's career.''

"Why?''

"Because Scott Fritche dated and then dumped Leo's cousin Melina. She's a student nurse here at the med center and was heartbroken when—''

"Sheely, this is not an episode of *General Hospital*. Please spare me the details of who's dating and dumping who. I'm only interested in the welfare of my patients, and right now I'm trying to ascertain whether—''

"All right. Fine,'' Callie said coldly. "Never mind gathering all the facts and coming to an informed conclusion. It's clear that you've already made up your mind.''

"Sheely, you are—''

"I'm tired of talking about this,'' Callie said, boldly cutting him off.

She turned and stalked from the lounge.

"Sheely, come back here.''

She ignored his command and stormed inside the empty women's locker room. Mercifully, it had not gone the unisex route like the lounge. Each sex still had separate quarters to shower and change clothes.

Moments later a tall, pretty blond nurse joined Callie in

an aisle of lockers, by the long bench positioned in the middle. "Sheely, Trey Weldon wants me to tell you that he has to talk to you. He said 'right now.'"

Jennifer Olsen had been in the class behind her in Tri-State's nursing school and currently worked in the obstetrics clinic, surrounded by expectant mothers. Jennifer made no secret of her ultimate goal, which was to have her own baby as soon as possible. Her more immediate goal, however, was to find a suitable man to marry and impregnate her. Preferably a doctor, with a sizable income.

At the same moment Callie wondered what Jennifer was doing up here in the women's surgical locker room, Jennifer must've felt obliged to explain her presence.

"I came up to see if Karen wanted to go to the Squirrel Den tonight. There's a bunch of us going."

Callie knew Karen Kaminsky, an OR nurse who'd graduated in Jennifer's class. "You must've missed her. She's probably at lunch."

"Oh. Hey, Sheely, you come to the Squirrel Den tonight, too, if you want, okay?"

Callie pictured the Squirrel Den, a relic from the city's industrial dark age, a dank, smoky, gloomy place jammed with cheap old tables and booths. "Uh, thanks, Jen. I'll try to make it," she said politely. *I just won't try very hard,* she added to herself.

"Sheely, about Trey Weldon, he—"

Callie sighed. "Tell him you didn't see me in here, Jennifer."

"But this place is too small for me not to see you. I wouldn't want to lie to the man."

"Certainly not," Callie murmured dourly.

Without a doubt Trey's credentials met, even exceeded, all of Jennifer's requirements in a potential husband and father. *Too bad, Jen,* Callie thought darkly, *you don't fulfill the prerequisites for Weldon class status any more than I do.*

Callie sucked in her cheeks and pointed at the window high above the lockers. "You can tell him I flew out that window on my broomstick. He probably thinks I'm capable of it. All I have to do is swap my surgical cap for my tall, pointy, black hat."

"The doctor is always right, and when the nurse doesn't agree, she's a witch, hmm?" Jennifer was sympathetic.

"Exactly. Just a doctor-nurse disagreement. It's nothing personal." Callie felt the need to stress that.

Although a little voice in her head pointed out that she was taking her inability to influence Trey in the Scott Fritche matter very personally, Callie instructed the little voice to shut up.

"Well, since he's waiting out there, I guess I ought to go tell him something." Jennifer lowered her voice conspiratorially. "Sheely, rumors fly around here, but I've never heard any about you and Trey Weldon. Still, I'll come right out and ask, and I hope you won't take offense. Are you two involved?"

"In what? A blood feud? No, not yet."

Jennifer giggled. "You know what I mean, Sheely. Are you and he, um, romantically involved?"

"No." Callie's heart lurched wildly. She would've liked to toss off a breezy quip about Trey being surgically gifted yet disabled in the art of romance, but the words stuck in her throat.

Because of the disturbing thoughts that flooded her mind.

For all she knew, Trey actually could be one of the world's great romantics, passionate, sensitive and thoughtful—yet extremely discreet. Possibly, he kept that part of his life so secretive that only the woman who was the object of his desire knew that side of him.

What would it be like, to know that there was a deeply secret, romantic side of Trey? *Oh, what she'd give to know!*

Thoroughly flustered, Callie forgot to breathe, and then had to inhale sharply.

"Sheely?" Jennifer's voice seemed to come from some other dimension. "Would you happen to know if Trey is going to the Springtime Ball?"

Callie jerked to attention. She was the one in the other dimension, a foolish one called fantasyland. Jen's voice came from the real world, and Callie's return to it was sharp and complete.

She heaved a small sigh. She was pathetic. Her hot, Trey fantasy, coupled with Jennifer's query about Trey and the big dance, was so junior high school she wouldn't be surprised to hear the bell ringing to change classes.

"I don't know, Jennifer. He hasn't mentioned the Springtime Ball."

"I know it's late, the ball is only two weeks away, but the guy I was going to go with had to cancel. He's a lawyer and has some stupid conference that just came up." Jennifer added quickly.

"I hate it when that happens." Callie tried to sound sympathetic.

"And I already have a dress and I *don't* want Joshua to think I'll be sitting at home that night because he can't make it. Maybe I'll just go ahead and ask Trey Weldon to the dance. Nothing ventured, nothing gained, you know." Jennifer smiled, a nothing-ventured-nothing-gained kind of smile.

Callie suppressed the urge to grimace. She fumbled with her locker combination, hitting the wrong number, having to start over again.

"See you later, Sheely," Jennifer called brightly, gliding out of the locker room.

Callie yanked the top of her scrub suit over her head, while dropping the pants to the floor. The suit was at least three sizes too big for her.

"Don't think you can hide in there and sulk, Sheely. You are going to listen to me."

"Trey, Dr. Weldon, you can't go in there!"

Callie heard the locker-room door open and slam hard against the tiled wall. She heard Trey's voice, angry and frustrated, followed by Jennifer's high-pitched protest.

But it happened so fast, in just a split second, that she didn't have time to process all the information until Trey was standing directly in front of her.

And she was standing in front of her locker, clad only in her white cotton bra and panties.

Trey seemed to freeze in place. Callie gasped and reached for her scrub top. She instinctively held it in front of her, shielding herself from his startled blue eyes.

Jennifer shrieked.

Two

Trey remained stock-still, as if he'd been turned to stone. It felt that way. He couldn't move, he couldn't speak.

He especially could not divert his gaze from Callie. So he just stood there, staring at her, watching as she snatched the scrub pants from the floor to hold them in front of her for additional cover.

But her alluring image already had been seared in his brain. In his mind's eye, he could still see the smooth bare skin of her belly, her legs, her breasts. Her belly was flat, her navel intriguingly deep; her legs were shapely, slender and well toned, her breasts pleasingly full.

Amazing how much detail he'd managed to absorb in those few burning moments.

He could accurately visualize her bra and panties, too, pristine white cotton, quite modestly cut. Plain, functional and practical underwear, the polar opposite of those sensual confections labeled lingerie, the stuff that was supposed to inspire male fantasies.

It seemed that Trey needed no such inspiration. Simply the sight of Callie Sheely in her serviceable underwear sent a shock wave of arousal through him so fast that within moments his body was hot and hard.

Instinctively he took a step closer to her.

"Trey, just in case you haven't noticed, you're in the women's locker room," Callie informed him through gritted teeth.

Trey's eyes widened and he was suddenly aware of the hyena-like screeching in the background. He cast a quick glance at the blond nurse, then looked back at Callie.

And blinked. "What?"

Callie groaned. "I feel like I'm trapped in an especially stupid episode of a very bad sitcom. I would've never thought *you* were capable of looking dim, but somehow you've nailed that 'huh?' the scene requires."

"I don't know what you mean," growled Trey, gathering his wits. It took longer than expected, and he blamed the surreal atmosphere. "I don't watch much TV and I certainly don't waste my time on bad sitcoms. And why would anyone bother to watch an especially stupid episode of anything?"

"Maybe to find a way out of a ridiculous situation—like this one," Callie said tersely. She shot a glare over his shoulder. "Jennifer, please stop screaming. Remember, he's Trey Weldon, not Dracula."

"Are you two having a big fight?" the blonde demanded a bit hoarsely. "A *domestic-dispute* kind of thing? Did he come raging in here after you, Callie?"

"Damn," muttered Trey. "Is that the story she'll spread all over the hospital?"

"Well, there's always the stock sitcom solution to fall back on," Callie murmured. "Shall I try it?"

Trey wondered if the dim "huh?" expression she'd accused him of had reappeared on his face. "Try what?"

"You took the wrong door by mistake, Dr. Weldon."

Callie's voice was clear and firm. "You made a wrong turn and ended up in here instead of the men's locker room."

"Oh sure, like I'm going to believe that!" Jennifer was scornful.

Trey couldn't blame her. "As excuses go, that's exceptionally poor, Sheely."

"Of course it is. That's the point, I think. The excuse is so dumb, it somehow works," Callie whispered back to him. "Or else the scene fades to a commercial break. Too bad we don't have that option now."

"What were you going to do to Callie, Dr. Weldon?" Jennifer's voice had a definitely accusing edge. "What would you have done if I hadn't been here?"

Trey decided her inquisition was worse than her shrieking, because the questions raised disturbing ones of his own. What would he have done if Jennifer hadn't been screamingly present?

He felt another flash of sexual heat streak through him. What in the world was happening to him? Here he was in the women's locker room, after deliberately barging in on Callie Sheely, not even caring that she had retreated to a place off-limits to him.

She had run off in the midst of their argument, leaving him frustrated and exasperated, but it wasn't as if he hadn't experienced frustration and exasperation before.

He had, plenty of times. It came with the territory when you were the smartest—and usually the youngest—in any class since the age of three. But for his feelings to turn physical, sexual, driving him to act impulsively like some kind of macho hothead...

Such behavior was totally uncharacteristic of him; he'd made sure of that. He saw himself as a thinker, a planner, a careful strategist, and that's exactly what he had become. Cerebral and controlled. The quintessential neurosurgeon, if one ascribed to the surgeons' personalities matching their specialties' stereotypes.

"He simply walked in here by mistake, Jennifer," Callie kept insisting. "Dr. Weldon is a brilliant surgeon, but he is pathetic when it comes to knowing his way around. He's always getting lost, takes a left when he should go right and a right when he means to go left. I think he could be classified as directionally challenged. Right, Trey?"

Trey almost automatically denied it. He had a superb sense of direction and prided himself on it. He'd had no trouble adapting to Pittsburgh's one hundred plus bridges crossing the three rivers, or to all the hills and winding streets, many of them one-way. He didn't bemoan the infamous lack of road signs that caused so many motorists, even lifelong residents, to get hopelessly lost. He didn't need them.

No, one thing he definitely was not, was directionally challenged.

He glanced down at Callie, about to lodge his protest. She rolled her eyes heavenward and grimaced.

"Oh, yes," he said quickly. "Right."

How could he forget, even for a split second, that Callie was making excuses for him, in order to convince the melodramatic Jennifer that she'd drawn all the wrong conclusions?

Which meant that once again he was faced with the question that plagued him, tantalized him, too. Without Jennifer's presence, just what would he have done with Callie Sheely?

Sheely, his ever-reliable assistant, his capable second-set-of-hands who'd stood before him, her bare skin so smooth and silky, her no-nonsense underwear covering more than it revealed, paradoxically inflaming him more than any racy black thong or see-through brassiere.

Trey swallowed, hard. "Sorry. I, uh, made a wrong turn. A mistake. I'm…distracted today." He turned and abruptly strode off.

Inside the women's locker room, Callie and Jennifer faced each other.

"He made a wrong turn, did he?" Jennifer said archly. "He came in here by mistake? So that's your story and you're sticking with it?"

"Pretty much." Callie shrugged. She hoped it appeared artless, that she seemed unconcerned.

Which she most definitely wasn't. Her insides were churning. She could still see Trey's intense blue gaze fixed on her. She could still *feel* his eyes on her, as if he had physically touched her. If Jennifer hadn't been here....

"I noticed that his shirt was inside out," Jennifer persisted. "Like maybe you'd been in the middle of—something physical—and then you ran away and he pursued you into—"

"We were in the middle of *neurosurgery* for the past six hours or so, Jen. You can check that out if you want. And I...I didn't notice his scrubs or how he was wearing them. It's not something I ever pay attention to."

Jennifer snickered her disbelief. "If you say so, Sheely."

Callie quickly snatched her sweats from the locker and pulled them on. She caught a glimpse of herself in a nearby mirror. Her body was lost in the baggy navy pants and Penn State sweatshirt, which she'd thrown on this morning for the drive to the hospital.

At 6 a.m. on a dark, chilly March morning, when she would go immediately to the locker room to change into OR scrubs, it didn't matter what she wore. She didn't care what she looked like now, either, Callie tried to convince herself.

So what if Trey was waiting for her outside the locker room and she looked shapeless and rumpled? Another glance in the mirror revealed her tousled bangs; her ponytail definitely needed to be brushed, too.

Well, she wasn't going to do it. She wasn't going to primp, because Trey undoubtedly wouldn't be out there waiting for her. He'd already done the unthinkable today by rushing in here after her. Cool, stringently self-disciplined Trey Weldon would never do the unthinkable *twice!*

What if he did? Callie's heart jumped.

Her dark eyes appeared feverishly bright to her in the mirror. Her cheeks looked as flushed and hot as they felt. Her lips were pale and bare, her lipstick long gone after the grueling hours in surgery.

There were two tubes of lipstick in her purse, but Callie wouldn't allow herself to retrieve either. She was not going to apply any makeup in the off chance that Trey Weldon might see her.

She grabbed her purse and headed for the door. "Bye, Jennifer." She hoped she'd achieved a credibly cheery tone.

"By the way, I'm not going to ask Trey Weldon to the Springtime Ball," Jennifer announced. "I am not the type who goes after another woman's man."

Jennifer thought Trey Weldon was her man. "As if," Callie murmured under her breath.

She tried to ignore the lonely little voice deep in her secret heart that cried, "If only." It was juvenile and silly and—

"Sheely."

The sound of her name stopped her cold. Callie whirled to see Trey standing beside the wall, just a few feet away from the locker room door. He still had his scrub shirt on inside out. Not that she paid attention to how *anyone* wore their scrubs.

Instantly a picture of Trey in his low-slung scrub pants, shirtless, flashed before her mind's eyes, clear as a photograph.

Too jittery to keep still, Callie started walking.

Trey fell into step alongside her. "I guess your friend is already cooking up some gossip that will speed through the hospital faster than a rumor on the Internet."

"You think?" Her lips twitched into a smile she couldn't suppress.

There was a civil war going on inside her, between euphoria—he had waited for her!—and her common sense trying to dispel it. For a few moments euphoria won, and she savored the sensation of walking beside him, their shoulders lightly brushing.

Until Trey moved a few steps away, making any accidental physical contact between them impossible. That successfully dissolved Callie's silly burst of joy.

"I apologize for putting you in a position that might possibly be misinterpreted, Callie," Trey said stiffly.

He'd called her Callie. For the first time.

She wondered if he was even aware of it.

Callie stole a furtive glance at him. She was always "Sheely" to Trey. During the entire year they had been working together, he'd called her nothing else.

Her surname was also used by most hospital personnel and had been since her nursing school days. It seemed that certain people were inevitably known by their last names while others were forever called by their first; Callie wasn't sure why, but that's the way it was.

She was pondering this, along with how odd yet wonderful "Callie" sounded coming from Trey, when he spoke again.

"I created—an embarrassing situation, Sheely. I don't blame you for being angry." Whether intentional or not, his voice held a cajoling note.

Callie realized that he had misinterpreted her silence.

"I'm not mad at you," she blurted. "Actually, when you stop and think about it, the whole thing is pretty funny."

"Hilarious," Trey muttered. "Can't remember the last time I laughed so hard. That woman's screams were a virtual comedic highlight. And my ears are still ringing."

"That woman?" Callie repeated drolly.

"I think I met her before, but I don't remember," grumbled Trey. "Should I?"

"Her name is Jennifer Olsen, and she was about to ask you to the Springtime Ball when you came charging through the door like a...rhino in scrubs."

The taunting sound of her voice was as disconcerting to

Callie as the words themselves. They had tumbled out before she'd had a chance to censor them.

"Ask me to a *ball?*" Trey looked aghast. "Give me a break, Sheely."

"You don't like to dance?" Callie dared to bait him. "Or you don't know how?"

Insight struck. So this was why she'd mentioned the ball and Jennifer's near invitation...in the hope that Trey would react exactly this way, appalled at the prospect. He didn't want to go with lovely, tall, blond Jennifer. Callie tried hard not to look pleased.

"I can dance." Trey was grim. "It took four miserable years of Miss Martha's Ballroom and Etiquette Classes, but I mastered it."

"Miss Martha's Ballroom Classes, plus etiquette, too," repeated Callie dryly. "I learned to dance watching the older kids at teen night at the VFW hall. It was pretty easy, but then, we didn't have to master the intricacies of ballroom etiquette."

"Not just ballroom etiquette. We also had to learn these arcane rituals that might have been relevant a century ago but—" He sighed. "I understand the necessity of instructing youngsters in the basics, and knowing how to dance is useful I suppose, but I swore that as an adult I would never subject myself to further torture along those lines."

"Miss Martha must have run those dance classes like a gulag commandant. Dancing is supposed to be fun, not torture."

"Is it?" he challenged. "Do you think dancing is fun, Sheely?"

"I guess it all depends on who you're dancing with," Callie heard herself reply.

And was promptly horrified with herself. *She couldn't have said something as blatant as that!* Why, she sounded like her ditsy sister, Bonnie, a compulsive flirt since the age of ten—and probably the least-subtle flirt in the universe, too.

Having watched and winced over Bonnie for years, Callie had made a studied effort to be her opposite. To hear herself throw out such an obvious come-on line made her cringe.

Worse, she could feel Trey studying her, his expression unreadable.

She was certain he was patronizing her when he replied in cool, measured tones, "And who do you like to dance with, Sheely? Scott Fritche?"

"I've assisted Scott Fritche in the OR from time to time. I don't dance with him."

"But you'd like to?"

"Oh, please, give me credit for having a little taste. Scott Fritche dates teenage student nurses. Any woman over twenty-one is too mature for him. He's a perpetual adolescent."

"Well, Fritche is sounding less and less like neurosurgery material." Trey frowned, his mind back on the surgical track. He seldom left it for long.

Callie was inordinately relieved. She'd come close to making a fool of herself with Trey, not that he seemed aware of it. One of the advantages of his never taking any personal notice of her, she decided wryly.

They reached the bank of elevators at the end of the corridor and could either leave the OR floor or go back to where they'd come from, the lounge and locker rooms adjacent to the operating and recovery rooms.

Trey glanced at his watch. "We do the astrocytoma with the laser in less an hour."

Callie nodded. "The patient is Doug Radocay. I, uh, mentioned that his grandmother lives in my old neighborhood near my parents' house."

"Yes, you mentioned that. Among other things that I won't go into. Feel free to thank me for my restraint, Sheely."

She was fairly sure he was kidding but not sure enough. "Thank you," she replied seriously. "It's very diplomatic of you to resist bringing up...those other things, especially since we agreed to disagree on them."

"If you say so, Sheely." Trey arched his brows. "Did I tell you that I happened to overhear you on the office phone when you bullied Mr. Radocay's HMO into approving the referral to me? They were against it, but you persuaded them to loosen the purse strings and pay up. You were impressively alarming, Sheely."

"I was simply following your lead, Dr. Weldon."

"Were you?"

"Uh-huh. I asked myself what would *you* say in a similar situation since you always manage to make those pencil-pushing bureaucrats on the end of the line bow to your will. I imitated your technique, right down to the blood-chilling tone and not-too-subtle threats."

"Thank you. And let me return the compliment, Sheely. In proper form, you too can freeze the blood of the pencil pushers."

He pressed the call button to summon the elevator. "I'm grabbing a bite to eat from the cafeteria. Are you going there?"

"I guess." She glanced down at her less-than-flattering outfit. "I meant to bring my lunch and eat in the lounge today but I forgot it. I, uh, I didn't expect to be seen in public looking like this." She shifted uneasily from one foot to another.

"You look fine," Trey said, as if on cue.

Callie's head jerked up. "That wasn't a bid for a compliment."

But it had sounded that way, she chided herself. "I look like a slob and I know it," she added sternly.

The elevator arrived, and they stepped inside the empty car.

"Let me put it another way, then." Trey pressed the button for the cafeteria located in the basement, and the doors snapped shut. "A suitably *un*complimentary way. You don't look any worse in that getup than you do in those oversize scrubs, Sheely." He grinned. "Better?"

Callie stared up at him. Trey didn't smile often. Quiana had once accused him of rationing his smiles, and he had somberly agreed that he was not the smiley sort. Therefore his grin—teasing, lighthearted—packed a potent wallop.

She felt slightly dazed. "Those scrubs are marked One Size Fits All. I've often wondered 'all' of what?"

"Gorillas, maybe?" suggested Trey.

"So if you happen to live on the Planet of the Apes, they really would fit all."

"And be worn in simian ORs," murmured Trey, his lips quirking, as if picturing one.

He successfully warded off the impulse to smile again. "We need to eat and get our blood sugar levels up. We're verging on giddy." His face was devoid of any further trace of amusement.

"Don't worry, Trey. Nobody would ever accuse you of being giddy, or even verging on it."

She glanced up at him, and their eyes met again. Callie tried to suppress the frisson of heat that raced through her. Trey looked calm and collected, and immaculate as usual, despite the grinding hours of surgery and disconcerting locker-room scene. Not even his inside-out scrub top detracted from his aura of dignity.

Callie ran a self-conscious hand along her bedraggled ponytail and then attempted to smooth down her bangs. Even with a concerted effort, could she ever acquire a tenth of the elegance that Trey seemed to naturally possess?

The elevator lurched to a stop and the doors opened. A crowd was waiting to board. The cafeteria was only a few yards away, and Trey and Callie walked toward it.

"Sandwich line?" he suggested. "Since Swiss steak is today's hot special."

"Sandwich line, definitely. Their Swiss steak is only for the very young and foolish, with ultrahardy digestive tracts. I remember eating it during my student nurse days, which are long gone—along with my ability to consume Tri-State's Swiss steak."

"You're not that long out of nursing school, are you, Sheely? You look like a kid."

"Thanks, I think. But I haven't been a kid for a long time. I'm twenty-six," she admitted. "As of last month," she added, because being twenty-six was still hard to fathom.

There had been a time when twenty-six seemed ancient to her. Now that she'd actually reached it, it did not feel old at all.

You're on the wrong side of twenty-five now, Callie, her sister, Bonnie, had joshed, as Callie blew out all the candles blazing on her birthday cake. Bonnie, four years younger, still considered twenty-six to be ancient.

"Last month? Uh, happy birthday, Sheely. Belatedly."

Callie didn't bother to respond to the perfunctory wishes. She knew very well that he had no interest in things like staff birthdays; he'd made it his personal rule not to participate in the inevitable collections for cards and/or cakes.

"Twenty-six." To her surprise, Trey picked up the thread of their conversation. "That's still young, Sheely. At least it is to me. I'll be thirty-three in October."

He looked slightly astonished by the fact, and Callie knew exactly what he was feeling.

"You're very young to be regarded as a respected authority and leader in your field," she pointed out. "But that's to be expected since you graduated from college in less than three years and medical school in only—"

"You've been reading the med center's press releases about me, Sheely. Gearing up to hit me for a raise?"

Callie blushed. If Trey only knew how much she knew about him, had read about him…he would probably peg her as an obsessed fan!

"I just wanted to remind you that you're still considered the Boy Wonder around here."

"Boy Wonder," he repeated. "That was my identity for a long, long time, but once you're thirty, you stop being a boy anything."

"Some men don't ever stop being boys," Callie said, with a touch of acid. "No matter how old they might be—which goes to prove you don't have to be young to be foolish, I guess."

She thought of Scott Fritche and his penchant for young student nurses, of her brother, Kirby, a year and a day younger than her, a self-described slacker living rent free in their parents' basement while he pondered what he wanted to do when he grew up.

"You're right." Trey looked thoughtful. "And it works the other way, too. Kids can be quite sagacious. I was, and I'm sure you were too, Sheely."

"Well, I never actually saw myself as a 'sagacious' sort of girl," joked Callie. And if she had been one, it was too bad she'd grown up to be a foolish woman, she added silently, one harboring a futile, unrequited crush on the unattainable Trey Weldon.

"Don't make light of your accomplishments, Sheely. I don't believe in false modesty. You were the valedictorian of your high school class and of your nursing school class, too. Those are not the accomplishments of a foolish girl."

"How did you know about all that?" She had never mentioned her scholastic achievements to him, though it was hardly a secret if anyone cared to check.

"I checked, of course. Before I offered you the position as scrub nurse on my team."

"You told me at the time that you'd been observing me in the OR and my experience there was why you—"

"I also checked your academic records, Sheely. I wanted to make sure you were the real thing, the complete package.

Knowledge and character supported and enhanced by skill. I had no intention of choosing anything less for my team.''

"Oh, that's me, the complete package.''

Grabbing a tray, she took her place in the sandwich line. There was a backup at the grill, with only one short-order cook working today, when at least three were needed.

Knowledge and character supported and enhanced by skill? Trey could very well have been describing Sister Benedicta, the stalwart principal of her old alma mater, Guardian Angels High School.

Could he make it any plainer? She did not evoke any romantic feelings within him at all. Callie unsparingly faced the truth: her insipid crush on him was even worse than hopeless, it was just plain absurd. Thank heavens nobody knew.

And then she thought of the glint in Jennifer's eye in the locker room earlier.

I am not the type who goes after another woman's man, Jennifer had said. Hadn't her expression been just a shade too perceptive?

Callie flinched, imagining the speculative gossip that might already be spreading via the ever-efficient hospital grapevine. When confronted, would a breezy laugh of denial be enough to counter the rumor, or should she offer some sort of explanation?

"You are, you know,'' Trey said quietly.

Callie's train of thought, already derailed by the probability of gossip, wrecked completely as Trey came to stand closely behind her.

Her senses seemed to take over, making her intensely aware of everything about him. Of the feel of his chest brushing against her back. Of the size and strength of his muscular frame, which seemed to surround her.

When she inhaled, his scent filled her nostrils with a musky mix of male sweat and pungent, antiseptic OR soap.

The temptation to lean into him, to press back against the

hard heat of his body was so fierce that Callie came dangerously close to giving in to it. To throwing caution and restraint aside and acting on her feelings, showing him that there was more to her than knowledge and character supported and enhanced by skill.

There was desire and need, and it was all for him. What if she were to take a chance and let him know?

"Dr. Weldon." A male voice sounded behind them.

Callie jumped and turned her head to see Scott Fritche approaching Trey. Hot color suffused her skin, right down to the tips of her toes. Her head abruptly cleared. She was herself again, and she offered mental thanks that she had not—impulsively and unprofessionally—nestled against Trey. She was horrified by her near lapse in sanity.

"Fritche." Trey frowned at the younger man who'd joined them. "I intended to talk to you sometime today. I suppose now is as good a time as any."

The pair left the line, and Callie abandoned the wait at the grill for the cold sandwiches that were already prepared, wrapped in plastic and set in ice near the cash register. She saw Quiana and Leo at a table with some general OR nurses and, pasting a smile on her face, she joined them.

One limp tomato and cheese sandwich later, she was back in the OR with Trey and the rest of the team for Doug Radocay's laser surgery.

As usual, there was a crowd of students observing; Doug was lightly sedated and dozed while Trey related his case history.

"This twenty-eight-year-old was on his daily morning run last month when he had a seizure for the first and only time. He went to his family doctor, who found no adverse neurological symptoms or brain abnormalities. It was concluded that the patient had become dehydrated from running, but as a precautionary measure, seizure medication was prescribed for the next six months. No further intervention was considered necessary. Any questions?"

There was a momentary silence.

"Um, then how did the patient end up here?" one of the medical students asked quizzically.

Trey's eyes met Callie's. "Good question. I'll let Callie Sheely here answer it. Sheely?"

"Me?" Callie was nonplussed.

This was a first. The operating room was Trey's showcase.

"I want you to tell the part you played in seeking further treatment for this patient, Callie," Trey explained.

Callie again? This time Callie caught Quiana's eye, and the other nurse teasingly waggled her eyebrows.

Callie cleared her throat. "I've known Doug, the patient, all my life. He's the grandson of a neighbor, Mrs. Radocay, who told my mother that she, um, felt that Doug's seizure hadn't been...thoroughly investigated."

Best not to mention that old Mrs. Radocay was known as the neighborhood psychic and her "feelings" and "hunches" were taken very seriously by everybody. If Mrs. Radocay felt something was dangerously wrong with her grandson, there must be.

Callie hadn't told that part to Trey, not until after the more advanced, detailed MRI had been given to Doug, confirming the presence of an undetected tumor.

Trey had complete confidence in the machine's technological findings, but gave no credence at all to the psychic connection. He ridiculed it, along with Callie's willingness to believe. They hadn't actually "agreed to disagree" on psychic phenomena, as she'd claimed earlier; they'd merely ceased discussing it.

"My mother asked me to ask Dr. Weldon to see the patient, and he agreed," Callie continued blandly.

No need to include how she had nagged and cajoled Trey for almost three weeks before he finally agreed to see Doug. How had she managed to do it? she wondered yet again.

Trey Weldon didn't do anything he didn't want to do—and he hadn't wanted to see Doug Radocay.

I completely concur with the diagnosis and treatment already prescribed. It would be a waste of valuable time to see this patient, Sheely, he'd said.

Will you see him anyway? Callie remembered asking, at least once a day. *Please?*

She'd persisted, all the while feeling it was hopeless. And then Trey had finally, astonishingly, given in to her request, and here they all were. Their eyes met again, and for a moment she almost believed he knew what she'd been thinking.

"Um, do you want to take it from here, Dr. Weldon?" Callie asked in her best nurse-deferring-to-the-doctor tone.

"Thank you, Nurse Sheely," he responded, his tone so dry that she knew he was mocking her, that he hadn't forgotten her distinctly undeferential "going to fire me?" dare.

Trey went on to explain that the more thorough and exacting computer imaging known as an MRI had revealed the germ of an astrocytoma, a deadly type of brain tumor. "This case is quite rare because the tumor was diagnosed at the earliest possible stage."

"Let's hear it for worried grandmas," piped up one of the residents.

"Yes." Trey cleared his throat. " We will monitor this patient for years, of course, but his prognosis is excellent...."

The procedure was fast and successful, and Doug Radocay was wheeled into Recovery.

"Sheely, you're coming with me to talk to this family," Trey ordered, catching her wrist as she headed toward the locker room, flanked by Leo and Quiana.

He drew her back, his hand moving to her elbow.

"Spooked by the thought of meeting the psychic granny, Trey?" Leo kidded. "Hopefully, she left her turban and crystal ball at home."

"Mrs. Radocay isn't a circus fortune-teller, Leo," Callie

said, shooting him a reproving look. Mentioning old Mrs. Radocay's psychic abilities to Leo definitely had been a mistake.

Still holding on to her, Trey pulled off his surgical cap. Callie removed hers, too, shaking her ponytail loose, trying not to stare at the beguiling sight of his long, elegant fingers wrapped around her arm.

Together, they headed for the stairs, the quickest way to the waiting room, located one floor below.

"I had wondered if you would mention the grandmother's, er, vibes to the students in the OR," said Trey as they trotted down the stairs.

"Aren't you glad I didn't? It would've been embarrassing for you if your scrub nurse was revealed to be a New-Age nutcase."

"I don't get embarrassed in front of students, Sheely. It's a waste of energy."

"You still don't believe that Mrs. Radocay *knew* there was something seriously wrong with Doug, do you? Even though the scientific evidence proved her right."

Trey's grip on her arm tightened. "The scientific evidence proved her right, but it was a lucky coincidence, Sheely. I'll bet the grandmother is an overanxious type who has worried about Doug his entire life and after thousands of false alarms—"

"She finally made a positive hit?" Callie laughed. "Like the Law of Chance or something? Is that how you've rationalized this case?"

"Well, you've turned it into an X-file," he countered.

"I thought you didn't watch TV."

Trey let her arm go as he opened the door of the stairwell. "I said I didn't watch much TV. I occasionally watch certain programs."

"But never the especially stupid episodes."

He paused and smiled down at her. "No, Sheely, never those."

His smile took her breath away, and for a moment they stood together, their eyes locked.

The sound of footsteps clomping down the stairs broke the spell. Trey and Callie jumped apart, like a pair of guilty teenagers.

"Callie, I just saw Doug in recovery." Jimmy Dimarino, first-year surgical resident and Callie's longtime neighborhood friend, came racing toward her. He lifted her off her feet and swung her around. "He's going to be okay! Thank God! Oh, Callie, ever since I heard about his brain tumor..."

Jimmy set her back on her feet and hugged her close. There were tears in his eyes. "I couldn't stop thinking about him. Remember how we used to play spotlight tag and hide-and-seek when he'd come over to visit his gran? And Doug was the one who showed us how to—"

"If you'll excuse me, I'd like to talk to my patient's family." Trey's voice was hard.

Callie and Jimmy looked at him, realizing at the same time that they were standing in the doorway, blocking it. Blocking Trey Weldon from passing through to convey the good news to the Radocay family.

"Dr. Weldon, I'm so sorry." Jimmy stood back, mortified. He extended his hand to shake. "I'm Jim Dimarino and—"

"I know who you are," Trey interrupted coldly, ignoring the proffered hand.

He'd seen the strapping, dark-eyed young doctor hanging around Callie too many times to count, had observed the pair talking and laughing together in the hospital corridors, the cafeteria, the gift shop. *Enjoying each other's company a little too much.* The decidedly petulant observation ricocheted through his head. Trey immediately tried to squelch it, along with the queer sense of deprivation assailing him.

"Jimmy and I grew up together," Callie said, to fill the sudden tense silence. "Our families are good friends and still live in the old neighborhood and..." Her voice trailed off.

She flushed. She was babbling. And Trey looked impatient, which he undoubtedly was. Not to mention bored with the trivial information about her and Jimmy that had come pouring out of her.

"I've watched you operate a number of times. Dr. Weldon," Jimmy interjected gamely. "I really wanted to see the laser surgery today, especially since it was Doug, but I was stuck in an appendectomy! I—"

Trey brushed by him without a word and strode briskly down the corridor toward the family waiting room.

Callie and Jimmy exchanged glances.

"Uh-oh." Jimmy groaned. "I think he's mad. Did I tick him off, Callie?"

"He's in a hurry to talk to the family." She didn't feel like dissecting Trey with Jimmy. "Come on, let's go see the Radocays."

She grasped Jimmy's hand, and they walked to the waiting room at the end of the corridor.

Three

Trey had already conveyed the good news of the successful laser surgery to Doug Radocay's parents, fiancée, brother and grandmother and was accepting their joyous thanks when Callie strolled into the waiting room, holding hands with Jimmy Dimarino.

Trey stopped speaking in midsentence. The Radocays didn't seem to notice. They were all talking at the same time, crying and hugging each other. When Callie and Jimmy joined the group, they too hugged and were hugged in return.

Trey stepped back and watched, composing his expression carefully, deliberately, into one of detachment. At least he hoped that's what it looked like, because he did not feel detached.

Far from it. Instead of being able to mentally remove himself from the surrounding situation as he usually did, to erect the protective wall between himself and what was going on around him, he found himself plunged into an unfamiliar torrent of emotions.

Anger ripped through him, intertwined with a maddening, helpless sense of confusion. The sight of Callie Sheely and Jimmy Dimarino seared him viscerally, as if he'd been struck by bolts of white-hot lightning.

He was jealous! And despite his longtime determination to avoid wild, deleterious emotions, he couldn't suppress this. Jealousy. He felt sick with it.

He hadn't yet recovered from that first bruising wallop, seeing Jimmy Dimarino pick up Callie and hold her close. Observing the obvious, comfortable intimacy between the pair. Now he'd been struck again, and he was feeling things he'd never felt before. Territorial, possessive...jealous!

Trey's lips twisted into a sardonic, self-mocking smile. This was a first. Having been blessed with the intelligence and talent to accomplish his chosen goals, even to surpass them, the Boy Wonder-Doctor-Hero previously had no one or nothing to be jealous of.

As for sexual jealousy...

He had certainly never fallen into that nasty trap before. Sexual jealousy included elements of passion and angst and wild desire—an upheaval requiring far more energy than he was willing to expend on any one person.

His less-than-passionate, jealousy-free past romances flipped rapidly through Trey's mind. His social life had always followed a comfortable pattern that precluded messy states such as jealousy; he'd made sure of that.

From adolescence, he had surveyed the pool of available, appropriate females and decided which ones he was attracted to. The chosen female inevitably returned the attraction, leading to a monogamous relationship—which never lasted too long. Usually he was the one to end it, but occasionally the woman herself would call it quits, citing his reluctance to make things permanent.

He'd never minded who acted first. His ego was as uninvolved as his emotions. For to be fair, mere *reluctance* didn't describe his unwillingness to wholly commit himself to a woman. *Refusal* was a more accurate term.

And refusing to even consider a permanent relationship didn't go over very well with women, most of whom were marriage-minded, he had come to realize.

Marriage was on his eventual agenda but not until he was forty, though he'd learned to keep his timetable to himself. Announcing it invariably evoked laughter from men and irritation from women. Nobody believed it was possible to make such a decision and stick to it.

Trey knew they were wrong. He would marry at forty, according to plan. Not a year, month or week sooner. His bride would come from a proper family with impeccable roots, she would move easily within the gracious world of the Weldons.

Let others flirt with unsuitable choices; let others plunge into impetuous wedlock. Trey never intended to make such mistakes. He had only to remember what his mother had told him about *her* first marriage and to compare it to her second more-mature and very happy union.

"I know you saved my grandson's life, Doctor." The voice of the grandmother, a small woman with warm, misting eyes and a deeply lined face, ripped into Trey's rambling reverie.

She took his right hand between both of hers. "Good hands," she murmured. "Hands trained to heal the sick."

Trey was uncomfortable. He understood the gratitude his patients' families felt, but he didn't want to be worshipped as a prophet. It happened, sometimes, and he always tried to put his role in the proper perspective.

"Mrs. Radocay," he began, about to modestly disclaim supernatural powers.

"Ah, but you don't want to talk about Doug right now," old Mrs. Radocay said, cutting him off. "Not when your head is filled with Callie."

Trey reacted as if she'd jabbed him with an electrical cattle prod. "I'm not sure what you mean, Mrs. Radocay," he exclaimed, visibly starting. Practically choking as he gasped for air.

"I am willing—eager—to answer any questions you have concerning your grandson's condition." It took a concerted effort to keep his tone level, professional. "I'm sorry if I've given you reason to think otherwise."

"Never mind, I understand," Mrs. Radocay replied kindly. "Callie is a dear girl. It's about time she found the right man. How do they say it—her Mr. Right?"

Trey felt hot as fire. He realized that he was sweating, he was breathing heavily, too. "You've drawn the wrong conclusion, Mrs. Radocay. Callie Sheely and I work together, we're not involved, uh, personally."

"It's all right." Mrs. Radocay patted his hand soothingly. "I see how it is. The minute Callie walked in here, you swallowed her up with your eyes. And you looked ready to toss poor Jimmy right out the window. Don't you worry, Doctor. Callie and Jimmy are old friends with lots of memories between them and nothing more. You want her, you'll have her."

She seemed to be issuing a decree. And instead of laughing it off, Trey was thrown into a panic.

He wanted Sheely? No, that was wrong. It was unacceptable. Ridiculous. He could not want Sheely; he refused to allow himself to want her.

But the jealousy, the bolt of desire in the locker room…

And what about the need he had to touch her? Not even to himself could he deny that he touched her frequently, his hand on her shoulder, on her arm, but this was the first time he recognized it as a need.

Trey gulped, feeling defensive. So he touched her often? Those were small, impersonal touches, devoid of hidden meaning, merely the familiarity of co-workers sharing time and space.

Like walking companionably together, as they'd done earlier today after the locker-room debacle. He remembered how his body had lightly grazed hers, their shoulders brushing, their fingers lightly touching....

He had instantly moved away from her, out of contact range—and he had blocked it all, both the thoughts and the sensations.

He'd had to, because the sensual electricity that rocked him had not been companionable at all. It had been erotic and alluring, too dangerous for him to acknowledge. Desire that strong did not fit in with his plan to wed at forty—he knew it.

Nothing was blocked now. He was flooded with sensations, with emotions, primitive and fierce. Still, he wasn't about to stop trying to contain all those messy, inconvenient, disturbing feelings!

"I'm afraid you're mistaken, Mrs. Radocay," he insisted, his tone urgent. It seemed imperative to convince her, as if doing so would compel her to withdraw her charge of him wanting Sheely. Then he could go back to not dealing with it.

"You see, it's impossible. I have an ironclad rule of never becoming involved with anyone on the job. There are, er, certain consequences, things like, um, lawsuits." It was a reasonable scenario, Trey rationalized, so why did it sound so stupid when applied to Callie and him?

Mrs. Radocay clearly thought so, too. She was visibly amused. "I'm sure Callie won't sue you, Dr Weldon."

Trey shook his head. "It's even more than that," he said desperately. "We're from two different worlds, and differences in background are—"

"Two different worlds," Mrs. Radocay repeated, her expression shrewd. "You know a lot about that, don't you, my dear?"

The old woman's gaze had become knowing, as if those piercing, sharp eyes of hers were looking into his mind, divining everything he kept locked inside it. As if she knew his secret, that he was not biologically a Weldon, however perfectly he seemed to fit the family mold—and he'd made it his life's goal to do just that.

Mind reading was impossible, Trey insisted quickly, stubbornly; he didn't believe in any kind of paranormal nonsense. But it was imperative that he extricate himself from what was fast becoming one of the most unnerving conversations he had ever been dragged into. "Mrs. Radocay, I must excuse myself and prepare for rounds."

"I didn't mean to scare you, Dr. Weldon." Mrs. Radocay looked contrite. "Especially not after what you did for our Doug. I thought you knew how it is between you and Callie, but I guess you don't. Yet." She patted his hand again. "And it's not what we're born into, it's what we make of our lives, but you don't really believe that. Yet." She turned to walk away.

"There is nothing between Sheely and me, and there won't be," he muttered.

But old Mrs. Radocay had rejoined her family and didn't hear him. Trey bolted for the door. He had to get out of there.

"Had more than enough adulation?" Callie caught up with him in the corridor.

"Something like that," Trey said grimly.

"I figured. I know I have. Doug's older brother called me a goddess—which would elevate you to the status of Second Coming." She smiled, slightly out of breath from having to run to keep up with him. "You have your get-me-out-of-here-right-now expression."

That diverted him. "What?"

"The expression you get when someone gets too chatty and bores you."

"Are you saying that I was rude to my patient's family, Sheely?" he snapped, his voice rising. It felt good to express his anger, especially at her. Especially since *she* was the cause of it! ''That I was glaring at them, that I ran out on them?''

Callie looked taken aback by the force of his anger. ''No, I just meant—''

''Spare me, Sheely. I know what I heard.'' Trey hurried up the stairs, Callie at his heels. He stopped dead at the top of the stairs and whirled around to face her. ''Why are you following me?''

Startled, Callie stumbled and would've fallen backward if he hadn't caught her around the waist to prevent the accident.

His grip tightened, and he lifted her off the stairs to set her on the landing beside him. She was so small, so light. It was like picking up a doll, and he felt a masculine satisfaction that probably had genetically evolved from primal, cave ancestors. He'd watched Jimmy Dimarino pick her up and wanted to dismember the guy but now, now *he* was the man with Callie. The man lifting her, holding her...

''I wasn't following you,'' Callie said breathlessly. Her eyes darted down to his hands still resting on her waist. ''I wanted to check on Doug and then go to the locker room to change out of my scrubs and go home. Since both Recovery and the locker room are on this floor...'' She swallowed hard, her voice trailing off.

Trey stared down at her, his eyes holding hers. As if of their own volition, his fingers were beginning to stroke the slender hollow of her waist.

You want her, you'll have her. Old Mrs. Radocay's voice echoed in his head, seemingly urging him on. Encouraging him to pull Callie into his arms, to kiss her sweet, slightly parted, beautifully shaped mouth.

He suddenly remembered a wild, passionate dream he'd had, more than once, about that mouth. But upon awakening, replete but sheepishly embarrassed, he had forcefully repressed the woman featured in those dreams. The repressed memory chose this moment to spring to his conscious mind, intensifying his desire, amplifying his need.

The woman in the dreams had been Callie. His mind, always so controlled, so sharp and disciplined, became blurred and unfocused.

"Trey, what's the matter?" Callie's voice, soft and husky, affected him viscerally.

What a sound! He looked down at her face, her mouth. What a sight! He wanted her so badly it suddenly seemed pointless to fight it.

"This," Trey growled. "This is the matter, Callie."

He did exactly what he wanted to do, what the psychic grandma had given him license to do. What Callie wanted him to do, because he saw her own desire and fascination and urgency shining in her big dark eyes.

Slowly, inexorably, he drew her to him and lowered his head at the same moment that she lifted her chin, their movements perfectly synchronized. Which shouldn't have surprised him at all, he thought dazedly. They worked in the OR together with the same exquisite precision, attuned and connected. A kind of intimate unity.

And then he ceased to think at all. His mouth opened hotly over hers, and she rose to stand on tiptoe, to wind her arms around his neck and press herself even closer to him. She gave a small gasp when his tongue entered her mouth, exploring, exciting, arousing.

His hands on her body were as active as his tongue in her mouth. Exploring, exciting, arousing.

He slid his palms over her hips and arched her into the hard cradle of his body. Cupping the curves of her bottom, he kneaded the rounded flesh, then directed his hands to glide over her thighs. He felt the sensuous shudder that racked her body, and it incited him further.

He deepened the kiss and rubbed his body against hers, wanting, needing more, so much more...

Callie clung to him, swept up by his passion, his demand,

which exacerbated her own. It was like a romantic fantasy that she rarely dared to indulge in—even when she did, she felt guilty and nervous and would swiftly bring it to an end.

She'd learned it was best not to think about what could never be, and kissing Trey Weldon definitely fell into that forbidden category of wanting but not having.

But it actually was happening now, exactly what she wanted. Trey holding her, kissing her. And he was very, very good at it. Never before had kissing been as wonderful, as thrilling. She should've known, Callie thought dizzily. Whatever Trey did, he did well; he did everything better than anybody else.

Pure pleasure shimmered through her. It was intoxicating, the hard warmth of his chest crushing her breasts, the strength of his arms holding her tight, his powerful thighs sliding along hers, between hers.

She felt his hands caressing her, and the erotic sensations rocketing through her were thrilling, the intimacy of his touch felt so right. But not enough. Instinctively her hips arched into him, their bellies rubbing. She felt the hard, heavy bulge of his manhood throb against her, and a honeyed heat pooled at her center.

Her breasts swelled and her nipples tightened in a kind of exquisite sensual pain. She imagined him soothing them, stroking them gently with his fingers, wetting them with his mouth, the intrusive layers of clothing between them removed....

Abruptly, her knees buckled. She felt too weak to stand. Her body was telegraphing an urgent message to yield, to surrender. Trey held her, supporting her, keeping her upright while taking control of her.

Callie willingly ceded it. She clung to him, savoring his male strength, his passion, kissing him back with an intensity and ardor that matched his own. Deep between her legs the ache grew sharper and hotter, more concentrated and intense. Her inner muscles contracted involuntarily as he thrust hard against her. She was close but needed to be closer, she wanted more, more...

And suddenly, shockingly, it was all over. She was standing alone, her limbs so shaky she had to grab on to the railing to hold herself up. Callie whimpered softly, protesting the cessation, the loss.

The railing was cold against her heated palm, and there was a chill in the stairwell that sent shivers through her. She wanted to be back in Trey's arms, she wanted him to hold her. She needed his warmth, his strength and his passion, too.

Callie drew a deep, ragged breath. "Trey?" She hardly recognized that whisky-toned, sexually raw-edged sound as her own voice.

Trey had moved away from her to stand against the opposite wall. His eyes held a feral glint as he looked at her, and she felt heat radiate from her body in waves, so intense he could surely feel it.

She saw him take a step toward her and willed him to come to her with every fiber of her being.

But then, as abruptly as he'd snatched her into his arms and kissed her senseless—and as abruptly as he had cut things off and moved away from her—she saw him shut down.

His eyes turned ice-blue, his expression distant. "That shouldn't have happened."

Only the uncharacteristic rasp in his voice betrayed any inner turmoil. Otherwise, he appeared cool and unaffected, his usual self.

Callie's heart turned over in her chest. Her body was screaming for more touching, more kissing but her heart yearned for something else. Simply a warm look from him would do, perhaps a few words of affection...

Was it too much to hope for an admission that what had just happened between them was right and wonderful and natural? That given their feelings for each other it was obvious—it was absolutely necessary!—that their year-long association should progress to a whole different level.

She gulped. What if it wasn't mutual, that his feelings didn't match hers? That this explosion of passion between them held entirely different meanings for each of them?

It seemed depressingly possible. At this moment Trey certainly didn't look like a man dazed by the wonder of...well, anything at all.

"It won't happen again," Trey announced fiercely. "I can only offer a—sincere apology for stepping way out of line."

Callie froze. *Apology?* Frustration and mortification roared through her, transforming the passion into fierce, feminine rage.

"Save it, Trey. I don't need an apology. Am I expected to apologize to you, too?"

"Of course not." He ran his hand through his hair until it was almost standing on end. "I take full responsibility. And I can offer no excuse. I only wish I could find an excuse for why I—for what I— I simply can't imagine—" He broke off abruptly. "I don't want to talk about this anymore. It's pointless."

He stared at the ceiling, the ground, at the wall.

Anywhere but at her, Callie noted bitterly. The back of her throat burned.

"Yes, it is pointless. Never mind offering any excuses, just take your...your full responsibility and...and—"

She was tempted to tell him just where he could shove his full responsibility, but she decided to take the high road. To get this back on track—the track that Trey had chosen without bothering to include her in the decision.

It was unfair! she railed inwardly. There had been two of them in that kiss, exploding into passion, but he had taken over, allowing her no opinion, no input. And now she wasn't even supposed to talk about it anymore because he had decided the urgency flaring between them was *pointless!*

But then, that was the way it was between them, wasn't

it? He was the master, the one in charge, and she was his paid lackey. Except now she was also his rejectee. He couldn't imagine why he had kissed her; he found it unfathomable.

Callie swallowed her hurt and concentrated on feeling insulted instead. It was more empowering. She would play this his way; to do anything else was to humiliate herself even further. Her instant, passionate response to him had already given away far too much.

"You're right. This shouldn't have happened, and it won't happen again," she said tersely.

She started toward the door to the floor, keeping her eyes away from him. She felt the sting of tears burn her eyes, and knew if she didn't get out of there immediately, there was a very real possibility that she would burst into tears.

That would certainly not go over well with the gifted doctor who had made it clear that he greatly regretted his impulse to kiss her. Who had decided that he couldn't even imagine *why* he had kissed her.

She should've suggested temporary insanity as his excuse, Callie mused darkly. After all, why else would the godlike Dr. Weldon bother with Nurse Nobody?

"Callie, listen."

Perversely, now that she was about to leave, he grabbed the door and blocked it, stopping her.

"Sheely," she corrected.

He stared at her, nonplussed, and she wondered if he even realized that he'd used her first name again. His confusion almost melted her angry hurt. This man could get to her like no one else ever had. And that wasn't a good thing. She even had to remind herself she was furious with him.

"We don't have any more surgery scheduled today and I want to leave now," she said coldly. "I have things to do. I do have a life outside this place, you know."

Too much, Callie scolded herself. *You are showing him way too much.*

And, of course, Trey was smart enough to interpret it. The man was a bona fide genius, after all.

"Sheely, we can't confuse our professional relationship with something else."

He was calm and controlled now, totally the prudent, rational doctor. The robotic one devoid of passion, the correct one who would never grab a woman, especially not his scrub nurse, in a moment of hot sexual urgency.

Callie tried to imitate his detached cool. "We certainly can't," she agreed in a tone so severely reasonable she almost scared herself.

Was it possible for a person to physically implode from suppressed rage? It was best she didn't stick around and find out.

She reached the door, expecting him to step aside and let her pass.

Trey didn't move. Now they were standing close together again, nearly touching.

Callie took a deep breath to steady herself and wondered if it was possible to smell the scent of heated sexual tension? Because if it was, she was definitely inhaling it.

"So we'll...forget this ever happened, Sheely?"

Callie stared up at him. She wasn't surprised to see that he wasn't looking at her, that his eyes were again fixed on a focal point far above her head. But that odd note in his voice was surprising. It sounded strangely like a...plea?

No, Trey Weldon didn't plead, she decided crossly. He gave orders—and expected her to follow them.

"Sure. Consider me amnesiac." She knew she sounded flippant, even bratty. *Good!* "Now, if you'll just let me by, we can—"

"Because workplace romances are notoriously stupid," Trey continued, not budging an inch.

It was Callie who took two steps back. Then three. "How true."

"And I have never been stupid in my life."

Callie heaved an irritated sigh. "Is this going to be a rehash of our 'young and foolish' conversation in the cafeteria? Really, there's no need. Being 'sagacious,' I remember it quite well."

He didn't seem to hear her. "We work well together, and I respect your ability as a nurse, Sheely. That goes without saying."

"Then don't say it," snapped Callie. "Just shut up and get out of my way!"

He gaped at her as if she'd grown another head. Callie conceded that she might have gone a tad too far. Telling her boss to shut up and ordering him out of her way made her "going to fire me?" challenge sound like a playful request.

"You see, this is exactly why I said what happened between us was a huge mistake." Trey's face was taut and red from the strain of maintaining his iron control. "Why it can never be repeated. Once a certain line is crossed, it is—"

"You're right," Callie blurted out. "And you don't have to fire me. I'll resign from your team. It's the only thing to do."

She turned and ran back down the stairs, escaping through the doors to rejoin the Radocays in the visitors' lounge. She knew Trey wouldn't return there, not that she expected him to follow her.

True, they'd crossed a "certain line" but she suspected that wasn't what disturbed Trey the most. It would be his loss of control, which he would find intolerable, and she fully expected him to hold her solely responsible. He would consider their impulsive tryst in the stairwell to be all her fault and would accept her resignation with relief. Callie had no doubts of that.

By tomorrow he would have convinced himself that he had narrowly escaped the clutches of a low-class conniver, using her wiles to advance herself to his exalted plane. He was already thinking it, she'd seen it in his eyes.

After spending a few more minutes with the Radocays, she headed directly to the director of nursing's office to tender her resignation from Trey Weldon's handpicked neurosurgical team.

Four

Callie usually enjoyed the quiet privacy of her small apartment, located on the second floor of a renovated turn-of-the-century house just a few blocks from the medical center complex. It was quite a contrast to the noisy rowhouse in the old neighborhood where she'd grown up and had lived until getting her own place nearly two years ago.

But now, sitting on the sofa in her combined living and dining room, the TV tuned to *Headline News* reporting one complicated world mess after another, the solitude seemed oppressive. Depressing. She couldn't sit still.

Though the area wasn't very conducive to pacing, she did it anyway, walking over to the tiny kitchen tucked into one corner of the big wide room, into the small bedroom off to the right, the even smaller bathroom to the left. And around her small table for two, where she ate her meals in front of the old bay window.

Her stomach was churning, her heart pounding. If she

were the type to suffer anxiety attacks, this would come close to qualifying as one.

She'd quit her job!

Callie mentally reviewed her race to the director of nursing's office an hour earlier. While Ellen McCann was always accessible to the nurses, some advance notice was usually required. But as fate would have it, the director had been free to see Callie the moment she appeared in the office. To look on as Callie wrote out her resignation with a shaking hand.

Callie requested to be reassigned to the general OR staff, listing "personal reasons" for leaving Dr. Weldon's team. When Mrs. McCann asked if she would like to discuss it, Callie said no and mumbled an excuse as to why not.

The rapid turn of events still stunned her, even though she'd set them in motion herself. She'd impulsively quit her job after insulting her boss...*after making out with him in the stairwell!* And now she was left with a sinking feeling that her behavior in the director of nursing's office had been—well, maybe a bit rash.

Callie pictured the impassive expression on the director's face as she babbled that she had to quit the Weldon team *right now* but couldn't talk about it. That she had to go home *right now*. Because she had a family emergency that she wasn't able to discuss at this time.

Callie cringed, just thinking about it. She was unable to discuss the faux emergency because she couldn't dream one up on the spur of the moment. She had the feeling Ellen McCann knew it, too.

Even now she couldn't think of a family emergency which would require her to leave work but could not be revealed to her boss. Why had she said such a dumb thing? It made no sense, especially following her unexplained resignation.

She was no good at lying, and it showed.

She had been even worse than rash, Callie decided glumly. Her behavior had been downright irrational. *De-*

mented also came to mind. She imagined the note Mrs. McCann must be writing in her personnel file. *Flake, airhead...* Did they use those terms in personnel files?

After torturing herself awhile, Callie's characteristic practical side began to emerge. Ruminating over what had already taken place was useless. She needed an alternative to staying here, grimly pacing and driving herself crazy. She would go home. There was always something there to distract her, and she needed the diversion. Badly.

Callie drove to the old neighborhood, which, like so many in Pittsburgh, was bound by a hill and a river, the streets steep and narrow and lined with houses so close that if someone sneezed in one kitchen, neighbors on either side called out, "Bless you."

The neighborhood also had a sprawling cemetery on the third side, isolating the area even more. Since there was no playground, and the schoolyard was nearly two miles away, generations of kids had played in the cemetery among the towering oaks and gravestones, including the current batch.

Callie literally ran into her sister, Bonnie, as she entered the house, and Bonnie was making a hasty exit.

"Callie, want to come to the Big Bang with me?" invited Bonnie. "It's Leather Night and women get free drinks till midnight."

Callie noticed that Bonnie was wearing various items of black leather clothing and a pair of handcuffs as a bracelet. "Uh, thanks, but I think I'll pass."

Bonnie clambered down the wooden steps, then stopped abruptly at the bottom and looked up. "I almost forgot. That doctor called, you know, your surgery boss. He said if I saw you I'm supposed to tell you to call him."

Callie's eyes widened. "Trey called here?"

"Trey?" repeated Bonnie. "So now it's *Trey* and not Dr. Whatever-His-Last-Name-Is? Wheeler or something?"

"Weldon. And why would he call here? Where did he get the number?" Her voice rose with every word.

"Duh, Callie. We're listed in the phone book." Bonnie jangled her handcuff bracelet. "What's going on? Something interesting?"

"A patient with an intracranial aneurysm is scheduled for surgery," lied Callie. She didn't want Bonnie to find her or Trey Weldon interesting. "Dr. Weldon probably wants to confirm some preop stats." Callie ordered herself to stop trembling.

"Oh." Bonnie's eyes were already glazing over. "Well, just remember, I gave you the message to call him back. He told me to tell you that at least five times in the three seconds I talked to him. Is he a slave driver or what?"

"Yes," murmured Callie.

Not that she was going to call Trey Weldon back. The *Titanic* would reemerge fully intact from the bottom of the sea before she called Trey Weldon. "Uh, have fun tonight, Bonnie."

"I always have fun," Bonnie assured her. She tossed her head, artfully swinging her long dark hair, a sexy, tantalizing move she'd practiced and perfected. "*You* should have some."

"I am going to have fun, Bonnie." Her younger sister's blatantly doubtful look inspired Callie to improvise. "Tonight a group of us from work are going to the Squirrel Den."

"Really? Well, the Big Bang is more exciting, but the Squirrel Den is a good enough place for you to start having fun," Bonnie said encouragingly.

"Any advice for a beginning fun seeker?"

"You're asking me for advice? Wow, this is a first." Bonnie was incredulous for a full moment. Then she ran back up the steps to give Callie a quick, sisterly squeeze. "Okay, here it is. Tonight, forget you're perfect. Play it loose—if you know how," she added, doubt shadowing her face.

"I'm not perfect," Callie protested, but Bonnie was already headed to her car, laughing off her denial. "And I know how to play," she added, more to convince herself than Bonnie.

Trey stared at the neon beer signs that illuminated the windows of a seedy-looking bar not far from the hospital. The Squirrel Den was spelled out in red art deco letters. When a young couple came reeling out the door, the sounds of a hundred different conversations plus terrible bleating music and thick clouds of smoke provided a glimpse of the atmosphere within.

Trey recoiled. This was the type of place he hated, the kind he made a point to avoid. He had never seen the charm of stuporous drunks or their habitats. Such people, such places caused misery and he had vowed...

Deliberately he squelched his antipathy. Instead of leaving, he resolutely pushed open the door and went inside. His eyes darted to the jumble of liquor bottles lining the wall behind the horseshoe-shaped bar, then scanned the crowd. The place was packed.

He was wondering if the city's entire young-adult population had decided to party at the Squirrel Den tonight when he recognized a group of hospital personnel crowded around a couple of tables along the far back wall. And right in the midst of them, talking and laughing, was Callie Sheely.

Trey pushed his way through the crowd, his gaze fixed purposely on his destination. On Callie.

She looked completely unlike herself. Instead of her usual baggy sweatshirt or simian-size scrubs, she wore a bright peacock-blue top that was short and clingy, emphasizing the soft curves of her breasts.

Her hair was different, too, not the practical ponytail she favored during work hours. Tonight her dark hair flowed freely over her shoulders, moving when she did. The effect was eye-catching. Seductive and alluring.

She had beautiful hair. The thought jumped into Trey's head, astonishing him. He was not given to rhapsodizing over women's hair; he would have a hard time remembering the styles of past girlfriends if ever pressed to do so.

But something inside him knew he would never forget Callie's silky black tresses.

As he drew closer to the table, he noticed that her eyes looked even bigger and darker than usual. She was wearing eye makeup, though those bewitching eyes of hers needed no enhancement. She was deliberately taking unfair advantage of her every advantage. Resentment streaked through him, and it didn't help at all that he knew it was ridiculous.

His gaze lowered to her mouth, and he swallowed hard. There was no use pretending to himself that he hadn't privately rhapsodized over that mouth of hers, first in his dreams, lately in his waking moments, too. But tonight she'd applied a scarlet lipstick that heightened the sensual allure of those beautiful lips. The color, the full softness, issued an invitation, a promise...

He sounded as if he were composing an ad for a cosmetic company! Trey mocked, disgusted with himself. But if he'd turned trite, Callie Sheely bore a portion of the blame for inspiring such thoughts!

"Dr. Weldon!" The blond nurse, Jennifer Olsen, greeted him first when he reached the table. She turned her head to glance at Callie, whose jaw was suddenly agape. "I guess I can't say this is a surprise," Jennifer added dryly.

"No, it's more like a total shock." A visibly astonished Leo Arkis stood up, extending his hand in welcome. "Please join us, Trey. "

Two second-year pediatric residents, one male, one female, also jumped to their feet, deferentially offering their space to Trey. A somewhat awkward silence descended over the group, so cheerfully raucous only moments ago. Trey felt a bit like a school principal paying a surprise visit to an unruly classroom.

It occurred to him that this was the first time he'd ever socialized with the lower-ranking hospital staff, the residents

and the nurses. For a moment his mannerly upbringing surfaced, and he considered putting them all at ease, telling the
younger residents to keep their seats, that he would sit else-
where. But taking their place would put him right beside
Callie. Right where he wanted to be.

His sense of noblesse oblige abruptly dissolved.

Trey slid behind the table, into the chair next to Callie's,
which she was sharing with a petite redhead, one of the
general-staff OR nurses whose name he couldn't recall.

"Glad to see you, Doc," Leo spoke up again, breaking
the silence. "But are you sure you're in the right place? The
Squirrel Den doesn't seem like your kind of scene."

Trey settled himself in the chair. "What's not to like
about a place with smoke so thick the respiratory systems
of the regulars here are probably similar to coal miners suf-
fering from black lung disease?"

Silence fell once more. He'd meant it as a joke, but even
to his own ears his tone sounded stern, with a definite judg-
mental edge. Trey didn't care. If his presence put a damper
on the gang, too bad. They could blame it on Callie Sheely,
since it was *her* fault that he was here.

There were way too many chairs crowded around the
small tables, and not enough room to accommodate the
group unless they squeezed tightly against each other or dou-
bled up on the chairs. Already several women were sitting
on men's laps. Others, like Callie and the redhead, were
sharing chairs.

"It's certainly crowded," Trey muttered, purposefully
pushing against Callie. "But I suppose the intimacy is part
of the charm of this place?"

He pretended he'd been jostled, crowding himself even
more tightly against her. Her scent, a tantalizing aroma of
spice and powder wafted into his nostrils, displacing the ac-
rid smoky smell of the air. The feminine fragrance seemed
to unleash a primitive, aggressive impulse deep within him,

spurring him on to primitive, aggressive acts unworthy of a well-bred gentleman. Like pressing hard against Callie.

"You're practically pushing me out of the chair," she hissed under her breath.

She hadn't looked at him since he'd first joined the group, when she had given him that wide-eyed stare of...of what? he wondered. Astonishment? Irritation? Panic? He couldn't read her at all tonight, and his frustration mounted.

"You chose the battlefield," he growled. "It's too late to complain about it now."

"Me?" Her voice rose to a squeak. "I didn't—" Her words turned into a gasp as some new arrivals shoved in on the other side of her, tipping the chair she was sitting on. There was a sharp cracking sound as the old chair wobbled precariously, then abruptly collapsed.

If Trey hadn't caught her around the waist and held her steady, Callie would have landed on the floor, the fate of her red-haired seatmate. One of the burly orthopedic interns lifted the little redhead off the floor and plunked her down on his lap.

"Good plan," Trey said, and impulsively did the same with Callie, effortlessly transferring her to his lap.

Callie sat absolutely still, rigid with tension. Was she dreaming? No, she was definitely awake, so did this mean she was hallucinating? *Because she couldn't be here in the Squirrel Den sitting on Trey Weldon's lap!*

But that was precisely where she was. The broken chair had already been pushed aside, its space immediately appropriated by other people in chairs. Trapping Callie on Trey's lap.

His arms went around her, a necessary precaution to keep her safely in place.

It didn't mean anything...did it? They were simply sharing a chair in a crowded place, as she'd done with her friend Karen, before the wretched thing had collapsed.

Of course, there were a few pronounced differences—

which were almost inducing her to hyperventilate. Callie concentrated on regulating her breathing, not an easy task given the circumstances.

From the moment he'd appeared at the tables, she had gone into shock. *Trey Weldon here?* And looking better than a man had any right to, especially a former boss who also happened to be totally out of reach for ordinary people like her.

She'd never seen him dressed like this, either, in faded old blue jeans—*Jeans!* Who would've dreamed he even owned a pair? But he did, and he wore them well, the worn denim accentuating his masculine attributes in a way baggy scrub pants never could.

He'd also donned a white cotton T-shirt, another radical departure for him. She could have sworn that Trey's off-duty casual wardrobe consisted of nothing but traditional khaki slacks and polo shirts—only in classically conservative colors, of course. His small beeper, which he was never without, was the only familiar item on his body and was looped around his belt.

He was certainly acting out of character, as well.

One of Trey's hands curved over her hip, the other grasped her thigh. She could feel the warmth of his palms, the strength of his fingers through the cotton-lycra material of her black pants.

This was more physical contact than she and Trey had ever had. Well, it was, if you didn't count their kiss in the stairwell that should never have happened...and that Trey deeply regretted—a fact he'd made painfully clear.

Remembering the way he'd recoiled, his abject horror at kissing her, was like being doused with a bucket of ice water. Callie stole a quick, bitter glance at Trey.

He was the picture of cool composure, but she knew him well enough to understand that beneath his calm exterior was an alert intensity, an awareness of everything relevant to the situation. He was that way in the OR as he performed an intricate operation, focused and vigilant, ready to act instantaneously if need be. But in the OR she pretty much knew what he was going to do next. Right now she hadn't a clue.

Why was he here? Callie wondered, cross and confused, and more than a little panicky.

You chose the battleground, he'd said. And right now his expression definitely could be described as warlike. Which meant she was the enemy? An enemy he held captive on his lap....

The scene had become almost too surreal to comprehend.

"Hey, Trey, have a beer cooler," Leo suggested. "They're a Pittsburgh tavern tradition." He slid a mug big enough to substitute for a pitcher across the table to Trey.

Callie saw Trey glare at her own beer cooler, which she had nervously wrapped both her hands around. What else could she do with her hands while sitting on Trey's lap? Draping her arm around his neck was definitely not an option. And holding hands with him, as several other lap-sitting couples were doing, was also out.

So Callie clutched her enormous mug.

Trey noticed. "You came here tonight to get drunk!" His voice was low and accusing in her ear.

"I came to have some fun with some friends." She sounded sassy and fearless though she felt neither. But emboldened by her tone, she dared to ask, "Why are *you* here?"

She felt him clench his fingers around her, as if chaining her to him. Callie shivered.

"You know damn well why I'm here. And I'm infuriated that you dragged me into this dive."

"I didn't drag you here!" she exclaimed indignantly, loudly enough to be overheard, had anyone been paying attention. But no one seemed to be. And then it struck her. "How did you know I was here, anyway?"

"I called your parents' house, and your brother beeped

your sister who knew where you were. Why does your sister carry a beeper? Is she a doctor or—''

"Bonnie's beeper is mainly a fashion accessory," Callie cut in, momentarily diverted by the image of a Dr. Bonnie. "You tracked me down? Why?" Sitting on his lap, the heat of his hard, muscular thighs pervading her skin, was clouding her mind, her judgment, more than any quart-size beer cooler ever could.

Trey clenched his jaw, and his blue eyes were stormy. "Are you going to insist on staying here, or will you consider going somewhere more conducive to serious conversation?" he asked tersely.

"Serious conversation? About what?"

"As if you didn't know." He was grim.

"I *don't* know," she snapped. "Are you going to enlighten me, or am I supposed to guess?"

He heaved an impatient, exasperated sigh that rumbled through Callie; their bodies were so close, they almost seemed to be connected.

" I don't mind *enlightening* you," Trey growled. "This afternoon—you do remember this afternoon, don't you? Well, I—''

"We've said everything there is to say about that," Callie cut in. Her face flushed crimson, and her words ran together in a rush. One conversation she never wanted to rehash was the humiliating one in the stairwell this afternoon. "You're…insensitive…to bring it up," she added.

"Insensitive," he repeated caustically. "Is that the reason you gave the director of nursing for quitting my team? That I was *insensitive?*"

"You don't have to worry about your precious reputation being tarnished." Callie tossed her head, and her dark hair swirled just like Bonnie's in those much-practiced flirtatious moves, she realized. Except Callie's movements were not premeditated to achieve an effect.

Trey appeared affected, though. As if unable not to, he reached up to touch a strand of her silky hair.

Crossly she batted his hand away. "I didn't give Mrs. McCann a specific reason for quitting. I just quit."

"Yes, you just quit."

His nostrils flared, and for a moment Callie stared, transfixed. She'd thought flaring nostrils were strictly a literary device, not a real indicator of controlled anger. Now she knew differently and realized how tightly controlled Trey's anger was.

Well, he wasn't the only one who was angry, she reminded herself. "Yes, I just quit," she echoed, defiant.

"You acted irrationally and impulsively," Trey said in a pompous, dictatorial voice she'd never heard him use before. "Your behavior was completely unprofessional."

Callie had spent too much time accusing herself of exactly that, but his thoroughly obnoxious tone fueled her ire.

"So was yours," she retorted. "And you acted just as irrationally and impulsively as I did."

"That is patently untrue. *I* did not quit *my* job in a fit of pique."

"*I* was talking about this afternoon in the stairwell."

The words were out before she could stop them, before it had fully dawned on her that he'd been referring only to her quitting her job, conveniently ignoring their little interlude in the stairwell.

"Are you aware of how extremely inconsistent you are tonight? I had no intention of mentioning an incident that is best forgotten, but you did exactly that—after accusing me of being insensitive for bringing it up!"

His voice was stilted and strained, and somehow that irritated her even more than his imperious tone. Callie frowned. Never mind that mere moments before, she couldn't bear the thought of discussing their unprofessional, irrational and impulsive tryst in the stairwell. His oh-so-obvious regret about kissing her was too insulting to let pass.

"Naturally, you're taking up residence in the state of denial. How typical! Isn't that what all lords of the manor do when accused of fooling around with the hired help?"

"I am not— You aren't— It isn't—" Trey broke off, shaking his head. "I'm spluttering like an incoherent fool. And it's—"

"Let me guess…it's all my fault," Callie finished for him. "It's my fault you're slumming in this dive with your lessers tonight, my fault you're acting like an idiot. I'm clearly a toxic presence, so do yourself a favor and go home."

She shifted restlessly on his lap, too nervous and edgy and just plain mad to be able to stay still.

"I can't," he said hoarsely. "I won't. And for godsakes, stop doing that."

Callie heard his sharp intake of breath as she was squirming. Beneath her bottom, she felt…

Was that what she thought it was? Just to rule out his beeper, she brushed her hand over the small black plastic device clipped to the side of his belt. No, what she felt throbbing in his lap was definitely not his beeper. But could it really be…?

Driven by a combination of erotic curiosity and instinct, she moved again.

"Don't," Trey commanded in a whisper, insistent and urgent.

His breath was warm against her neck. A sensual shudder racked Callie's body, and she knew he had to be aware of it, just as she was aware of his very obvious arousal, hard and hot against her.

She wriggled again, knowing it was provocative—even inflammatory—but doing it, anyway. Would this qualify as "playing it loose," as recommended by Bonnie?

"Stop it, Callie," he ordered huskily.

His use of her name only spurred her on. "And if I

don't?'' Callie taunted. Baiting him. Once again she slowly, erotically moved her hips against him.

Yes, Callie decided, she was most certainly playing it loose. And what complicated everything was how very good it felt. All of it—fighting with him, teasing him, arousing him.

She heard his breath catch once more in the back of his throat, and a syrupy warmth flowed through her. That burgeoning bulge in his jeans had been inspired by her, and knowing it, feeling it, evoked her own urgent responses.

"Callie, if you don't...don't behave—"

"You'll fire me? Too late, I resigned, remember?"

"This isn't working." Suddenly, abruptly, the desperation left Trey's voice and he snapped to action. "We're leaving."

His voice rose as he stood up, bringing Callie to her feet as well. "We're leaving *now*."

Five

Callie felt Trey's arm around her waist, as hard and unyielding as a steel band. His other hand clasped her forearm just as firmly. She had only a moment to snatch her cardigan sweater as Trey half lifted, half carried her around the table.

It all happened so fast she had no time to marshal an adequate protest.

"Excuse me," Trey said to no one in particular, addressing the crowd as a whole. His tone and body language conveyed the far-less-polite demand, Get out of the way.

Everybody reacted instantly, jumping left and right to allow Trey, still gripping Callie, to make their way through the pack of partyers.

"'Night, Sheely. 'Night, Trey. Be sure you two crazy kids spend the night doing everything I would," Leo's teasing shout carried over the din.

Since Leo had never been shy about discussing anything, Callie already knew the wild and varied ways he spent his nights. She gulped for air.

Trey continued to walk her to the front door of the bar, his body shadowing hers, his hands holding her against him as he propelled her forward.

Her feet were barely touching the ground. "Let me go!" she commanded. "Stop right now!"

"And if I don't?"

He used the same baiting tone that she'd used to taunt him a few minutes ago, while sitting on his lap. Callie's heart seemed to stop, then start again at warp speed.

Trey didn't let her go, and she was aware of every inch of his muscular frame moving against her.

They reached the entrance, and Trey pushed the door open with his shoulder, retaining his grip on Callie as he hauled her outside. Compared to the noise level inside the Squirrel Den, the street was relatively quiet.

Trey released her, quickly moving several steps away from her.

For a few moments they stood together in awkward silence on the sidewalk. Callie pulled on her peacock-blue cardigan to ward off the damp night chill and noticed that Trey had no jacket. The sight of his bare, well-muscled forearms and strong masculine hands struck her as especially sensual.

"Where's your coat?" she blurted out. If he were wearing one, maybe it would be easier for her to focus on something else. "Aren't you cold?" she added weakly.

"Not at all. My anger has raised my body temperature to at least 112 degrees Fahrenheit. If it starts raining, the drops will boil as soon as they hit me."

She knew it was supposed to be a joke, but Trey's forbidding demeanor didn't invite any laughter in response.

"So this dump is where you choose to spend your off-duty hours?" Trey's eyes were fixed on her, watching her intently. "Helluva place you picked to go for *fun,* Callie."

Callie swallowed. Was this how a mouse felt when being observed by a purposeful cat? Plus, her overly feisty streak seemed to have run its course, leaving her practical, sensible self to handle the consequences. Well, she would try to inject a practical, sensible note into an otherwise chaotic evening.

"I'm sure the Squirrel Den is quite different from where you choose to spend your off-duty hours." She took care to keep her tone deliberately, carefully bland.

Her remark visibly annoyed him. Trey's frown deepened, his dark brows knit together, turning his expression into a classic one of disapproval. "And where do you suppose I choose to spend my off-duty hours, Callie?"

"Oh, no doubt hanging out at your country club."

"I don't *hang out* in country clubs," he replied testily. "I don't *hang out* at all. That implies loafing, wasting valuable time, which I make a point never to do."

"I wasn't trying to insult you, Trey. Nobody knows more than me how valuable your time is. I just meant that whatever it is you do at your country club—golf? tennis? black-tie dinners and charity balls?—any of that would be an extreme contrast to an evening at the Squirrel Den."

Country clubs. The Squirrel Den. Upper class, working class. Once again, the vast differences in their social stations struck her. Of course, the most insurmountable chasm of all was the vast differences in their feelings for each other.

She was stupidly in love with him, while he didn't find her acceptable even as a receptacle of his lust. He'd proven that by his rapid flight from the bar when his physical reaction to her on his lap became apparent. If she needed more proof, she could find it in his abject horror over their kiss in the stairwell earlier today.

Unrequited love was nothing more than a fantasy, ultimately unrewarding and disappointing, Callie silently reminded herself. If she required further proof of *that,* she need only look at the mess her life had become since this afternoon.

Being in love was a game for two players—a bit of wisdom from her mom that Callie herself had borrowed to quote to lovelorn friends through the years. How disheartening that she hadn't listened to her own warning!

Callie turned to stroll casually along the sidewalk, away from the Squirrel Den and from Trey. At least, she hoped it looked like a casual stroll, because she was trying hard not to give in to the powerful urge to bolt and run.

She needed to get away from him. Being around Trey Weldon, even when it involved arguing with him, was a pleasure she could not allow herself. She couldn't afford the emotional price.

But seconds later Trey was walking beside her.

"How do you know I belong to a country club?" he demanded, picking up the thread of their conversation.

"I guessed." She shrugged. "You do, don't you?"

Trey said nothing. His usual long-legged, fast-paced stride caused him to move ahead of her. He had to slow down and wait for her to catch up to him, then purposely take smaller steps to stay at her side.

Callie could only guess how much that must irk him. In the hospital, she was always the one keeping pace with him, even if it meant running to match his high-speed gait.

"I'm going to take your silence as a yes answer," she said dryly. "You belong."

"I like to golf, and my free time is too limited to spend waiting on a public course. Is that a crime?" Trey snapped.

"Of course not. I, um, bet you're a whiz at tennis, too."

"If I don't comment, will you take that as a yes answer?"

"I probably will."

She kept walking and so did he, still at her pace, much too slow for him. "Trey, is your—"

"I avoid black-tie dinners no matter where they're held," he cut in vehemently. "They're invariably dull. And I already gave you my opinion about dancing."

"Yes, I remember. You hate it and hold Miss Martha's

Ballroom Etiquette Classes responsible. But I'm sure those lessons have come in handy on the charity ball circuit.''

"You don't seem to have made the connection that hating to dance rules out going to balls," he said through gritted teeth. "And don't think I haven't picked up on your disparaging inflections, Callie. Are you accusing me of being a snob?"

"No." She shook her head. "Not at all. You're just being true to your origins."

"As if you knew," he growled.

Callie was tempted to say she did know. But wouldn't that risk revealing she'd read everything published about him in every Pittsburgh publication, that she'd committed to memory every fact she'd ever heard or overheard about him?

She had endured enough blows to her pride today without adding another, thanks very much. A change in subject was definitely in order. "Where are you parked?"

"What?" Trey stared at her, as if he couldn't comprehend the very simple question.

"Your car. Where is it parked? You are walking to your car," she added because he still looked uncharacteristically blank. "Aren't you?"

"My car is parked in the opposite direction. I'm walking this way because you are... And I know you know it, Callie."

Now it was her turn to stare, uncomprehending.

He heaved a sigh. "You aren't going to make this easy for me—you've already made that clear."

A swift jab of excitement pricked her, and she sensibly tried to counter it. "It would help a lot if you told me what you're talking about," she said carefully, keeping her voice steady, her tone light. Revealing none of her increasing inner turmoil.

Was it possible that she'd misinterpreted his reaction to what had happened this afternoon...and tonight? That maybe he wasn't averse to a personal relationship between them, after all? Being Trey, he would find it hard to admit, especially after his declaration to the opposite in the stairwell.

"This must be what is called eating humble pie," Trey grumbled. "Not a tasty dish."

Callie's heart thudded with anticipation and uncertainty. "Trey, whatever it is, just say it."

"All right." Trey pulled something out of the back pocket of his jeans. It was a piece of white paper folded into a square small enough to be crammed into a pocket. "Here it is."

Confused and unable to take her eyes off him, Callie watched in silence as he methodically unfolded the paper. She tried hard to tamp down her physical awareness of him, but it shimmered through her, enticing and strong, even as a sense of dread began to grow.

"Your resignation." Trey held out the paper with a flourish.

One quick glance confirmed that, despite the many wrinkles from its folding, the paper was indeed the copy of her resignation, which she'd tendered to the director of nursing several hours ago. Callie jumped back as if struck by a poisonous snake.

"Rip it up," Trey ordered. His hand reached out to grasp her wrist, and he shoved the paper into her hand.

Her fingers closed automatically around it. "Where did you get this?" she whispered, staring at her signature, which had been witnessed by the director of nursing, who'd signed it herself. "I gave it to Mrs. McCann."

"I know. And she gave it to me. She undoubtedly thinks we're both—well, to put it kindly—not quite acting like our normal selves today." Trey cleared his throat and looked away, studying the traffic light with apparent fascination.

"That is putting it kindly," Callie mumbled, forcing herself to look away from him. She pretended to stare at a parking meter with the same rapt attention Trey was bestowing on the traffic light. "Putting it more honestly, we've been acting like lunatics today."

"True, unfortunately," Trey agreed brusquely. "First you went racing into Ellen McCann's office to insist you were quitting your job with me on the spot. Then, within an hour, there I am, barging into her office, demanding to know if you'd actually gone through with your threat and resigned in the throes of a bad-tempered snit."

"Ohhh! You didn't say that to the director of nursing, did you?"

"Well, yes. She said you told her you were quitting for personal reasons and had assumed we'd had an argument. I...let her believe that. So when I asked for the copy of your resignation to give back to you, Ellen handed it over. She also suggested that we work things out between us. Er, professionally, of course."

"After all that, I can just imagine what kind of reference I'll get from Mrs. McCann when I apply for a job somewhere else!" exclaimed Callie, aghast.

"You don't need a reference from her, because you aren't leaving the hospital center or my team, and we both know it." Trey gave a harsh laugh. "The very fact that I tracked you to that rat hole tonight—and went inside!—proves that I intend to..." He took a deep sharp breath.

"Rip up that resignation, Callie."

Instead, she began to refold the paper as meticulously as he'd unfolded it, until it was again a minuscule square. She tucked it into a side pocket of her purse.

"You've called me Callie all evening," she murmured, looking thoughtful. "Why? Is your not calling me by my last name part of your effort to work things out professionally?"

"I don't always call you by your last name."

"You did until today."

"The, uh, stairwell incident?" He lagged behind a pace or two.

Callie didn't wait for him. "Before that," she called, over her shoulder. "The locker-room incident."

Trey flinched and came to a halt. So she'd noticed him practically slavering over her in her underwear? Well, how could she not? He certainly hadn't been subtle about it. As for when she'd become Callie and not Sheely to him...

A good question. One he wished she hadn't asked because it made him face what he'd prefer not to. Sheely. Callie. He'd managed to keep them separate entities—for a while.

Callie appeared only in his steamy erotic dreams, while dependable, sexless Sheely remained the perfect helpmate in the OR, so attuned to him she often seemed like a seamless extension of himself.

But at some point, he couldn't exactly pinpoint when, the sexy nighttime dream girl and his faithful daytime partner had fused into one and the same woman. A woman he admired and relied upon, needed and wanted. *That* had never happened to him before.

It was both exhilarating and terrifying, but he'd tried to keep a lid on his feelings. A mistake, no doubt. Because given the intensity of his pent-up desire for her, it was probably inevitable that an out-of-control scene like the one in the stairwell would result. Not to mention tonight, when he'd pulled her down onto his lap and held her, so desperate for her he never wanted to let her go.

Trey reminded himself of his life strategy, of his plans for marriage at forty to a carefully chosen proper wife candidate. Right now he was seven years off schedule.

Forty was the right age for him to marry; he was absolutely certain of that. Dad had been forty when he'd married. When his older brother, Winston, turned forty, the same year he married Parker Lee—whose proud lineage dated back to prerevolutionary Britain or maybe beyond—Trey was convinced his marital decision was eerily prescient.

But right now a future marriage at forty was a long time away. Right now he was watching Callie Sheely walk away from him. She didn't even bother to cast a glance back at him to see if he was following her.

Probably because she doesn't care if you are or not, taunted a snarky little voice in his head, a voice he seldom heard because he was too sensible, too rational, too basically indifferent, to wonder about women and their motivations.

He was wondering now. And drawing some disturbing conclusions....

True, Callie had responded passionately to him this afternoon, but she had also quit her job. She was royally ticked off: her sexual attraction to him had taken a back seat to her anger. After all, it wasn't as if she had professed her undying love for him.

The realization jolted him. Why, it was her rage that governed her behavior, not any desire to marry him! And here he was, behaving like a chump, getting panicky about marriage simply because Callie Sheely turned him on.

Just because he wanted to sleep with Callie didn't mean he wanted to marry her! And vice versa, of course. She would probably laugh in his face if he told her he'd been brooding about their kiss leading to marriage—that would be after she called him an arrogant snake or decked him. Perhaps all three?

Of course sex did not automatically lead to marriage! Why he had somehow forgotten that in regard to Callie was a question he didn't care to pursue. Not now, not watching her walk farther and farther away from him.

She hadn't ripped up that damnable resignation, either. She meant to go through with it. She was really serious about quitting her job with him, about leaving him....

A dark chill went through him, and it had nothing to do with his lack of a jacket. He'd been so sure he could convince Callie to come back to him. But she hadn't ripped up the resignation. She was still walking away from him. Trey felt a bleak inner cold that seemed to permeate every cell of his body.

"Wait!" He called as she was inserting a key into the front door of a large Victorian-style house set slightly back from the sidewalk.

Callie paused and turned to see Trey striding toward the house. She waited for him to join her on the small porch. He stood beside her, seeming to tower above her.

"Where are you going?"

"Inside. I live here." Callie pushed open the front door. "On the second floor."

There was a small entrance foyer with access to both a narrow front hall and a carved wooden staircase leading to the second and third floors. There were two apartments on each floor. Callie stepped inside and Trey came right in with her.

The heavy door closed behind them, automatically locking. The pair stood together in the dimly lit foyer. Callie nervously traced the inside of her lips with the tip of her tongue.

Trey stared down at her, his eyes following every movement. The sight of her little pink tongue wetting her lips sent a shock wave through his body, which settled well below his waist.

Say something! Do something! he commanded himself. *Don't stand here gaping like a slack-jawed dope!*

Trey moved toward her. He felt the overwhelming urge to behave in a way not at all in keeping with his carefully designed life strategy.

Callie took a step backward. And he advanced one forward. They were now at the foot of the staircase.

He braced one hand on the wall, striking a seemingly casual pose. "Aren't you going to ask me in for coffee?"

Callie knew him well enough to know that there was nothing casual about his stance or the fierce intensity burning in his blue eyes like a flame. Trey Weldon was not a casual type of guy, even in low-key situations. Which this one definitely was not.

She tried to stall while she decided what she ought to do. "Do you really want coffee at this hour? The caffeine will—"

"So make it decaf, I don't care. You were concerned about me being cold earlier. Well, a hot cup of coffee will warm me up, won't it?" He shifted, almost imperceptibly.

But the slight motion brought him closer, and he towered above her, hot and male and intense. Callie sucked in a breath. If he were to come up to her apartment, she could think of better ways to warm him up than serving him a cup of coffee.

So ask him up, an inner rebellious voice challenged. *Never mind what you ought to do, why not do what you want to do, for a change?*

"Please, Callie," Trey said quietly, his eyes meeting and holding hers.

Callie needed no rebel alter ego to encourage her this time.

"Come on up." She turned and started up the stairs.

When he asked her in that particular way, looking deep into her eyes, saying please, calling her Callie... She was lost and she knew it. Might as well be gracious in defeat.

Trey followed her up the stairs and watched as she used a second key to let them into her small apartment.

Which seemed even smaller with him in it. His masculine presence dominated the decor, a coordinated mix of floral patterns in pastel shades. There was an assortment of bright accent pillows piled on the sofa, an arrangement of silk flowers on her small coffee table, an old toy brown bear wearing a sweater on a toy-bear-size rocking chair in the corner. A shelf by the bay window held a number of well-tended plants in colorful ceramic pots.

She also had an eclectic collection of picture frames crowded together on a polished, round table. Trey went to them immediately, picking up one of her, Kirby and Bonnie aged five, four and one, respectively.

"You were a cute little girl," Trey said, looking from the picture of little Callie to the present-day Callie.

"Thank you." She smiled at the memory the old photo evoked: their mother dragging them to the photographer's, bribing them with the promise of ice cream if they behaved and smiled for the camera.

"That picture was the last time our mother ever dressed the three of us alike. Not long after, Kirby and I absolutely refused to wear anything similar to what Bonnie—a mere baby—was wearing. Now that we're grown up, you still couldn't pay me to dress like her," Callie added dryly, remembering Bonnie in Leather Night garb.

"Since my brother and I are ten years apart in age, there was never a question of us dressing exactly alike," said Trey. "Although, I wouldn't have minded it. As soon as I was old enough, I copied his style, borrowed his clothes. I always tried to emulate Win in every way."

"I knew you had a brother, but you've never said if he's older or younger. If you tried to emulate him, he must be older."

"Yes, by ten years. And I endured the misery of Miss Martha's classes only because Winston himself had been a student. One of her star pupils, actually."

Trey replaced the children's picture on the table, his smile fading as he spied not one, but *three* pictures of Callie and Jimmy Dimarino in a triple frame.

One showed them as small schoolchildren, missing their front teeth. In the middle photo they were beaming teens in high school graduation caps and gowns. The third picture was the most difficult for Trey to look at. It was a recent one of them as young adults, arms around each other and grinning.

In all three photos the pair looked as if they were enjoying their own private joke. Enjoying each other's company immensely.

Trey thought of this afternoon, after the Radocay laser

surgery, when young Dr. Dimarino had picked up Callie and swung her around, when the two of them had entered the waiting room, holding hands. The warmth and intimacy between the two was apparent, and now the presence of *three* photos of Dimarino here in Callie's apartment absolutely confirmed it.

Callie watched him uncertainly, wondering why he was glowering at her frame collection. A moment ago he'd been downright congenial, interested in her pictures, smiling, sharing little family jokes. And now...

"You look the way you do in the OR when a resident botches something. Do the pictures of my family annoy you?" She was only half kidding.

Trey didn't even half smile. "Let's not forget the special *friends* interspersed with the family photos."

"Are you insulted I don't have any photos of our neurosurgery team?" joked Callie, trying to jolly him into a better mood. "I figure I spend enough time with you guys as it is, so I don't need to see your faces when I'm off duty."

It was definitely the wrong thing to say. Trey's face grew as dark as a spring sky during a thunderstorm. "Well, you won't be seeing much of *our* neurosurgery team anymore. You quit, remember?"

"I'm not about to forget," she retorted. "I need to find a new job right away. Unlike you, I have to work for a living," she couldn't resist adding.

"As opposed to me, a dilettante who does neurosurgery for fun and only on a whim?" Trey instantly picked up on her little dig. His face was hard. "That's low, Callie. My work is my life, and you know it. You owe me an apology."

Callie looked ashamed for just a second, but then her defenses—and her temper—surged. "Don't hold your breath waiting for one. You're not my boss anymore, I don't have to...to pander to your ego anymore."

"That's it! That's enough!" Suddenly Trey lunged at her, and though she began a quick retreat, walking backward, he followed her. Across the living room, right through the doorway of her small bedroom.

The room was dim and shadowy, the light from the living room providing only slight illumination. Callie didn't stop to turn on the overhead light; she didn't even think of it, not with Trey advancing on her.

She backed her way right to the edge of her bed, Trey almost toe-to-toe with her. When she stopped, he abruptly halted in his tracks, his face, his body only inches from hers.

They stood there, their eyes blazing, their breathing fast and heavy.

"I—I'm sorry," Callie said at last. "That was low. I...I know your work is your life."

His breath stirred her hair; her rising breath lightly skimmed his lips.

"I'm sorry, too," he murmured. "The last thing I meant to do was to lose control of my temper and scare you."

He pictured that flash of fear in her eyes when he'd advanced on her, and the power of his anger made him wince. Years ago he'd made a vow never to become a raging, threatening bully. To rage and threaten a woman, *Callie,* meant that he—

"I'm not scared," Callie whispered, gazing up at him. "I know you'd never hurt me."

Trey saw desire shining in her beautiful dark eyes, without a trace of fear. The burn of his anger instantaneously transformed into a flare of passion; her words were a balm, enabling him to unleash it. He felt his sex swell impossibly fast and full, and he wrapped his arms around her, holding her tight, letting her feel his need.

"Yes," she breathed, in answer to the question he hadn't asked, at least not with words.

Six

"**I** want you so much," he managed to gasp.

He clasped the back of her neck, tilting her head, and took her mouth with his, hungrily parting her lips with his tongue. He filled her mouth, exploring it, claiming it with possessive urgency.

Callie moaned and stretched up her arms to clutch at his shoulders, clinging to him, satisfying the irresistible urge to press her breasts against the solid breadth of his chest, rubbing the tips against him.

He was iron hard and aching, and he grasped her bottom and rocked against her. Their hips writhed in tandem as their bodies were given over to an ancient rhythm, displacing their formidable self-control. Dissolving it.

Neither Trey nor Callie cared. It was too late to stop now. They sank onto the bed, arms and legs entangled, still kissing. Her black shoes slipped off her feet and hit the floor with a gentle thud.

She hardly noticed. Trey was caressing her, his hands

moving over her, sweeping the length of her once, then twice, before lingering to cup her breasts. He fondled the softness until she uttered a small cry of yearning.

He seemed to understand her unspoken message. They were close but not close enough. Trey slipped his hands under the hem of her shirt and deftly divested her of both her cardigan and top. He tossed them down, where they landed in a peacock-blue heap on the floor.

Callie's eyes met his, and she saw his gaze lower to her small, full breasts which were swelled and aching for his touch.

He murmured something unintelligible that sounded like "beautiful, even more than in my dreams." She knew she couldn't have heard him right; she must be wishfully interpreting his words, because Trey wasn't given to extravagant compliments. She wasn't beautiful, and there was no way he'd ever dreamed about her or her breasts.

For a split second she wondered if she were dreaming right now, if she was actually sound asleep, about to be blasted awake by her alarm clock.

Then Trey slipped his fingers beneath the waistband of her black pants, and his touch on her sensitive skin was too viscerally real to be a dream. Reflexively she sucked in her stomach to give him better access. She felt his fingertips skim her bare belly, dip into the small center of her navel and then move even lower to trace the lacy band of her bikini panties.

"Do they match the bra?" he asked huskily, one hand fingering the silk-and-lace blue cup of her bra while the other did the same to her panties, still concealed beneath her slacks.

"Y-es." She could barely breathe, let alone speak coherently.

"I want to see. And to not feel guilty for staring, the way I did this afternoon," he added, a bit sheepishly.

For a few moments the passion that had dazed her lifted.

Callie experienced a sharp flash of clarity, remembering her serviceable cotton underwear that he'd seen her wearing in the hospital locker room, a time that felt light-years away from this particular moment.

So much had happened since then—too much! And when she had bathed and changed for her night out, she'd never expected, never imagined the evening would end like this....

He kissed her again, and that potent combination of love and desire and need for him overcame her, sending all cautious reserve and inhibition back on hiatus. Callie completely surrendered to Trey and to her feelings for him. Heat and excitement surged through her, and she allowed herself the supreme pleasure of caressing him, of touching him as she'd always wanted to.

She smoothed her palms over the long, strong length of his back, she ran her fingertips through his thick dark hair while they kissed and kissed. Her tongue rubbed his, and she explored his mouth as thoroughly as he was probing hers, enticing and demanding.

"Callie, I can't wait any longer." Trey's voice was rough and raspy and sexy.

The sound of it affected her as fiercely as his kisses and caresses. "No more waiting." Her voice was a soft promise—and also a demand.

There was a hot throbbing deep in her abdomen that radiated lower and deeper. Her bra was swiftly discarded, and she arched upward as his lips closed over one of her nipples that had tightened into a taut nub of sensation. She felt the moist warmth of his mouth on her bare breasts and moaned with pleasure.

I love you, she thought, holding his head against her, gently stroking his hair. *I've always loved you.*

Unable to resist, she lowered her hands to the muscled tautness of his buttocks and clenched them through the denim. Emboldened by his responsive groan, she daringly moved one palm around to trace the burgeoning distension beneath his jeans. She felt a thrill of feminine power as he shuddered with the force of his arousal.

"Now," he urged, sliding from the bed to his feet to pull his shirt over his head with one swift tug.

He dispatched the rest of his clothes just as efficiently: his jeans, his belt with the beeper still attached, his socks, shoes and gray cotton boxer-briefs joined her growing pile of clothes on the floor.

He stood beside the bed, powerful, male and nude. Callie's eyes widened at the sight of him, urgent and aroused. She reached out her hand and closed her fist around him, gently squeezing.

He emitted a noise that sounded like a soft, explosive hiss. She glanced up at him, observing his expression of pleasure-pain, then extended her other hand, eager to excite him higher, to appease her need to touch him and further heighten his impassioned response.

But he moved so very quickly she was caught by surprise when he came to kneel behind her on the bed.

"Any more of that, and it'll be all over before we've even begun." The low rumble in his throat could've been either a chuckle or a groan.

His hands cupped her breasts and he kissed the curve of her neck. Callie melted back against him, closing her eyes, losing herself in the haze of swirling, thrilling sensations.

She turned her head, her lips seeking his, and they kissed. It was a kiss of warmth and affection, bonding them with its sweet intimacy, even as another tidal wave of passionate urgency crashed over them.

Trey hooked his fingers on the waistband of her black pants and pulled them down her legs, taking her panties with them. Her thin black socks went, too, and he kissed his way back up her legs, his hands stroking her calves, her thighs.

Carefully but purposefully, he moved her legs apart and nibbled on the inside of her thigh. Callie gasped and jerked, her spine arching. As though inspired by her frenzied reaction, he dipped his tongue into her fragrant nest of dark hair.

She cried out his name, her head tossing back and forth, her face flushed. It was too much, she wanted him to stop…but she would die if he stopped. She wanted this wild, wicked rapture to go on and on.

He didn't stop. Callie trembled, her fingers clutching and unclutching as his teeth gently nipped the tiny, taut bud signaling her own urgency and arousal.

She had never experienced such shattering, astounding pleasure. It radiated from her center, overtaking her, rendering her mindless. Suddenly she exploded into ecstasy, her body pulsing as wave after wave of sensual intensity bathed her in glowing warmth.

He didn't give her time to come down. His hands lifted her hips, positioning her to receive him. He entered her slowly, powerfully and inexorably. His groan of pleasure echoed in her head.

"You're so tight, so hot. You feel so good," he crooned softly.

Callie gulped a silent scream. She felt as if she were being stabbed, ripped apart as he filled her with his hard, searing heat. Her eyes filled with sudden involuntary tears, and she bit her lip to keep from making a sound.

Sheathed deep inside her, Trey braced himself on his elbows above her and gazed down at her.

"Callie, are you all right?" His voice had lost its dreamy resonance. He sounded serious, concerned.

She saw that his face was damp with perspiration, that his whole body was trembling from the strain of holding himself back. A surge of love flooded her, releasing the tension that gripped her inner muscles. Her body relaxed, melting into a honeyed warmth as it adjusted to his size and strength.

"I'm fine." She ran her hands over the smooth damp skin of his back, nuzzled the hollow of his neck and breathed in the scent of him. "In fact, I'm a lot better than fine. It's—good, Trey."

She realized it was true. She wasn't simply saying the words to placate him. The warm weight of his body felt wonderful on her...in her.

He brushed her mouth with his, then met her eyes. His were filled with concern, with understanding. "It's been a while for you." It was more of a statement than a question.

"You could say that." She smiled at him.

He returned her smile and then lowered his head and kissed her deeply. Callie responded with ardent urgency, giving in to the overwhelmingly sharp need to writhe beneath him.

"Yes. That's it, Callie." He lifted his lips and gripped her legs, raising them. "Just like that, sweetheart."

He began to move slowly at first, with deep, even strokes that grew deeper and longer and harder, quickening in pace. Callie clung to him, quivering as those hot waves of pleasure he'd evoked within her such a short time ago, again built and grew inside her.

She matched her movements to his, their rhythm in perfect sync, their timing exquisitely attuned to each other.

"I knew it would be good, I just knew," Trey rasped, his breathing harsh and rapid, his body slick with sweat. "Perfect. Together. The way we are in the OR."

His words affected her like the most potent aphrodisiac. *Perfect together.* Lying here with him, making love with him, seemed a natural extension of their on-the-job rapport. They really were perfect together in the operating room...and in the bedroom.

He claimed her mouth again, their tongues duplicating their bodies' actions. Swift and sudden their passion flared to flashpoint. And in their usual synchronicity, they reached the pinnacle of sheer physical ecstasy together.

They shared an intense, rapturous climax, suspended in bliss for timeless moments until they slowly, languorously drifted down from the heights together. Perfectly together, Callie thought dreamily when she was able to think again at all.

They lay on her bed, their bodies still joined, damp and exhausted, dazed by the stunning force of their passion, by the spectacular pleasure of its release.

Callie held Trey, stroking his neck, his shoulders, tracing the long fine line of his spine with her fingertips. He kissed her lips lazily, then pressed soft hot kisses to her throat, her breasts.

This glowing aftermath was almost as wonderful as the fire of their lovemaking, she thought, and wondered if she should tell him so. Or if she should say anything at all? The silence was nice, so restful and serene. Perhaps Trey preferred it to conversation.

But they really had a lot to talk about. And acknowledging this made her realize that ahead of them was a conversation she didn't feel like having.

The marvelous cloud of mindlessness began to lift. Though her body was deliciously replete, her mind was suddenly back on duty. Alert. Speculative. Reflective and anxious.

Eventually her body caught up with her mind.

"What's wrong?" Trey stirred, lifting himself up a little to look into her eyes. "You tensed. I felt it."

"Given our...position...I guess it's impossible to try to hide anything." She caught her lower lip between her teeth. It felt kiss swollen and moist from his mouth.

"You shouldn't want to hide anything," Trey reproved softly. "Now tell me."

Tell him. Callie gulped. Where to start? Should she tell him she loved him? Or would that be a mistake, since he hadn't mentioned the word *love* himself?

She closed her eyes. Should she mention that she'd been a virgin until tonight, when he had so expertly altered her chaste status? Since he hadn't said anything, maybe he hadn't noticed. It was quite a compliment for him to perceive her as experienced instead of an incompetent novice. Wasn't it?

Unless he was too polite to mention her lack of expertise. Callie's heart lurched in near panic, but almost immediately logic kicked in, calming her.

She certainly knew Trey well enough to realize that he was unable to let any mistake, anywhere, go uncorrected. If she'd done something wrong, even in bed, he would have spoken up immediately. It was ingrained in his nature.

But he had said it was good for him. That they were perfect together.

"Are you falling asleep on me?" Trey sounded amused. He kissed her forehead, then lightly brushed his lips along her hair.

Callie opened her eyes slightly and slanted him a glance from beneath her lashes. "That wouldn't be polite, would it?" Her voice sounded drowsy and slurred, even to her own ears.

"If you're about to segue into some wisecrack about Miss Martha's etiquette lessons, I won't be responsible for my actions."

This time her eyes flew wide open. Trey was grinning, his expression as playful as his tone. A playful, lighthearted Trey Weldon was not a sight often seen. Had she *ever* observed it before now?

It was wonderful to behold. Callie felt a special warmth suffuse her. She was deeply in love and deliciously satiated, feeling closer than ever before to the man she loved.

No, Callie decided then and there, she wasn't going to ruin the mood by bringing up such potential downers as virginity and an untimely declaration of her love.

"You not responsible for your actions? That doesn't work as either a threat or a promise, Trey," she teased gently.

She cupped his cheek with her hand, relishing the rough feel of his unshaven skin beneath her fingertips. "I can segue into *any* subject, and you'll remain totally responsible for your actions. You don't know how to be irresponsible, you couldn't be, even if you tried. Maybe it's an inbred Weldon trait."

"You couldn't have said anything that pleases me more," Trey said quietly. "Thank you."

He tightened his arms around her and dropped a quick kiss on her temple. Good thing she hadn't told him that he had deflowered her and that she was in love with him, Callie thought wryly. He had just unwittingly confirmed that wouldn't have pleased him. It appeared she couldn't go wrong praising the impeccable Weldon bloodlines, though.

Trey slowly eased himself out of her and rolled to one side. Callie's whole body felt chilled from the sudden loss of his warmth and weight, from the abrupt disconnection from him. She wanted to cry out in protest.

"This has been one helluva long day—all the ups and downs." Trey heaved a long sigh. "I haven't felt this beat since I was a resident." His voice trailed off. "Come here."

To Callie's relieved delight, he drew her into his arms, spooning her as they lay together on the bed.

"I don't like ups and downs, either," she murmured. "Neurosurgery provides enough excitement in my life, so on a personal level I try to keep things on an even keel. Just one of the reasons why my sister and brother consider me boring beyond belief," she confided shyly.

"You couldn't be boring if you tried, Callie. And I'll take an even keel over bouts of histrionics and melodrama any day."

Callie smiled. Trey felt the way she did; it was wonderful to understand and be understood.

She would have liked to share that particular insight, but they were both too exhausted right now for a soulful chat. Her eyes, already adjusted to the dimness of the bedroom, focused on the stream of light shining in from the living room.

"Maybe I ought to turn out the lights in the living room?" she wondered aloud.

"Doesn't matter." Trey already sounded half-asleep.

Warm in the circle of his arms, the length of his body heating hers, Callie decided to leave the lights burning. She felt his breath rustling her hair on the top of her head, heard his heartbeat thudding against her ear, providing a steady, hypnotic rhythm. She felt completely at peace in this private place they had created.

Her eyes drifted shut.

The sharp staccato sound of Trey's beeper woke them simultaneously. Both instantly sat up in bed, nearly knocking their heads together in the abrupt, confusing transition from deep sleep to wakefulness.

They stared at each other for a second or two as full awareness overtook them. The torrid memories were quick to follow. Their intense lovemaking, falling asleep in each other's arms in Callie's bed. And now, awakening naked.

Reflexively Callie clutched the sheet and pulled it to her neck, shielding herself.

"A little late for that, isn't it?" Trey murmured wryly. He tugged at the sheet, his intention to pull it away from her quite obvious by the gleam in his eye and his firm grip on the material.

Before either of them could say another word, Trey's beeper sounded again. It was on the floor, still looped over the belt in his jeans that lay among the scattered mixture of both his and her clothing.

He climbed over the bed to fetch it. Callie glanced at the clock—4:15 a.m. There must be an emergency concerning one of their postsurgical patients, and she tried to guess who it might be. No postop complications had been expected in any of them.

She watched as Trey glanced at the number on his beeper and then used her phone to dial.

His replies to the voice on the other end of the line mostly consisted of "Yes," "Uh-huh" and finally "Sure, of course. I'll be right there."

He replaced the telephone receiver in its cradle. "That was George Mercer."

"George Mercer, the dean of the medical school? Why did he call you?" Callie was bewildered, still not quite at peak functioning level.

"He was calling on behalf of Paul Hagen, you know, the chief of radiology at Tri-State. Hagen's fifteen-year-old son was just in a car accident. He and some other teenagers were drag racing on the parkway, going God-only-knows-how-fast, and the driver lost control of the car." Trey heaved a troubled sigh. "Crazy, reckless kids."

"According to Mercer, three of them are dead and four are in critical condition, including Hagen's son, who has severe head injuries. They're taking the boy into surgery, and Mercer asked if I'd go into the OR. He's asking all the department heads to consult on the Hagen case, as a courtesy to Paul."

Trey pulled on his clothes as he spoke. "From the way he described the accident and the injuries, the prognosis is grave."

Callie watched, concentrating on the facts he'd given, trying to get everything straight, though her body was urging her brain to forget it and go back to sleep.

"If the Hagen boy is only fifteen, why wasn't he taken to Children's Hospital? Kids under eighteen with those kinds of injuries are usually taken there, aren't they?"

"Yeah, that's where he is. They have their own trauma team there, neurosurgeons, too, of course, but Mercer is rallying the Tri-State staff. I agreed to go in tonight, even if I do nothing but observe."

Trey picked up her clothes that he'd taken off her earlier and tossed them to her. "Hurry up and get dressed, Callie. I said we'd be there right away."

"We? *Me?*"

She knew Children's Hospital also had their own staff of skilled operating room nurses who specialized in treating children and adolescents only. It was one thing for the medical center's CEO to request a courtesy consultation by a top-rated surgeon, but the presence of other nurses was neither needed nor asked for.

"If I have to do anything neurosurgically, you'll be there to assist me. Not that I think we'll be asked, since pediatric head trauma isn't my specialty."

"But maybe you *will* be able to do something for him," Callie said softly. "This boy is fifteen, not an infant or small child, and you've operated on quite a few teenagers with tumors and AVMs."

She thought of those cases, of how horrible it was for teens to face brain tumors and circulatory malformations, and how Trey's skill had given their lives back to them. Though he was certainly capable of treating grievous head injuries, he usually left that to trauma specialists, preferring to focus on brain anomalies.

"I don't mind going in now, even if it's just to offer support to the Hagens." Trey glanced at his watch. "It's fortunate we aren't scheduled for our first operation of the day till late this morning, so we have plenty of time for this."

"Only you would consider eight-fifteen to be late morning," Callie said wryly.

"It is. You know I consider 6 a.m. the ideal time to begin." Trey walked over to the bed, picked up her peacock-blue shirt and pulled it over her head. "Come on, sweetheart. Speed it up. We have to get going."

For a moment Callie's mind reeled as their two separate worlds and identities seemed to collide in the most surreal way. Trey, now in high gear as Dr. Weldon, was calling her "sweetheart" and helping her dress, as a lover would.

Callie decided there was no time to think about all that

now. She pulled on the rest of her damp, smoky clothes, grimacing. "These are really disgusting. Give me a minute and I'll change into some—"

"There's no time, we're leaving now." Trey picked up her shoes with one hand, caught her hand with his other and dragged her along with him, out the door, down the stairs.

He paused in the entrance foyer. "Damn! My car is parked over by the Rat's Nest."

"That would be the Squirrel Den. Not to worry, my car is parked right up the street, about a half block from here." Callie slipped into her shoes and took her car keys from her purse.

They walked in the predawn darkness to Callie's car. It was a shiny, electric-blue Neon, the first new car she'd ever owned. She was close to having it all paid off.

"Give me the keys. I'll drive." Trey walked to the driver's side and held out his hand.

Rather imperiously, Callie thought. "I'd rather drive. I— I'm kind of possessive about my car," she explained.

And due to her unrelenting policy of being the sole driver, her car had yet to have a dent or a scratch. She'd learned some useful lessons over the years by watching her parents hand over their car keys to the merrily careless Bonnie and Kirby. The Sheely vehicles invariably ended up looking like beat-up trash cans on wheels.

But Trey Weldon was anything but merrily careless, and Callie was on the verge of reneging on her ironclad policy when she noticed him giving her Neon a critical once-over.

"Possessive about this?" Trey snickered. "Why?"

Defensively, Callie laid a protective hand on her trusty little car. "Well, would you let me drive your Porsche?"

She'd heard Leo and other doctors speak reverently about Trey's six-month-old black Porsche Carrera. Apparently, it was the ultimate male dream car, and she was well aware that the odds of her ever driving it were on a par with winning a hundred-million-dollar lottery.

"That is a fallacious argument." Trey huffed his disdain. "The issue here is that I'm the faster driver, and we need to get to the hospital immediately."

"You've never driven with me, so you don't know who is the faster driver. I promise we'll be there within ten minutes. You couldn't get there any sooner unless you ran every stop sign. Which is *not* recommended if you want to arrive in one piece."

Callie brushed by him and climbed into the driver's seat, giving him no choice but to take the passenger's side.

She started the car as Trey folded himself into the seat beside her. He didn't say anything as she drove along the blessedly traffic-free boulevard toward Children's Hospital, which was in the same complex as Tri-State, but Callie felt his eyes upon her.

What did he see when he looked at her so intently? She wished she had more confidence, but was convinced she looked a fright. Her hair was disheveled; she'd barely had enough time to pull it into a ponytail. Their spontaneous passion last night had precluded removing her makeup, and the cold water she'd splashed on her face this morning hadn't helped much.

"I look like the before ad for virtually any product," she mumbled.

Trey chuckled.

"You don't have to agree with me," she challenged gingerly, and he laughed again.

Because he did agree with her and was trying to be tactful, Callie decided. No, she was not an object of any male's dreams this morning. She tried not to mind his honesty.

She pulled the car into the hospital parking garage and headed toward one of the many empty slots.

"Why don't you park closer to the elevator, Sheely?" Trey's suggestion sounded more like an edict.

Sheely. Callie's heart sank. So they were back to that? Well, she shouldn't be surprised. After all, they were back in the hospital environment, about to assume their professional roles again. She was even treating his parking directive as doctor's orders as she drove closer to the elevator banks and pulled her car into a nearby place.

Last night they had crossed the line from colleagues to lovers. A momentous step, but they'd had neither the time nor opportunity to discuss what had happened between them in bed. Callie wondered if they ever would.

It didn't seem very likely. Knowing Trey and his formidable emotional reserve, chances were good he would be willing, maybe even relieved, to leave their impromptu night of passion unmentioned. Unacknowledged.

After all, what was there to say? Callie sighed inwardly. She loved Trey, had given her virginity to him and didn't regret it. *Not yet, at least,* added that tiresome voice of caution, which she'd so successfully suppressed earlier in the night.

As for Trey, she knew he didn't love her, and he didn't know she'd been a virgin. At this point the best she could hope for was that he didn't regret making love to her.

Silently she followed him from the garage to the elevator connecting it to the hospital building. Trey, however, seemed inclined to make conversation.

"Are you always so hell-bent on driving?" he asked curiously.

"When it's my own car—always."

"So I noticed. That's why I didn't try to take your keys. When you say no, you mean it, don't you?" He seemed entertained rather than offended by his observation.

"Why is it when men say no, it's no, but if a woman says no, it means time to begin negotiating?" Callie retorted lightly as they stepped into the elevator. "I heard that asked on a TV talk show and asked myself the same question."

"We didn't negotiate who drove your car," Trey reminded her. "And you wouldn't negotiate ripping up that resignation, either."

He reached into the pocket of her cardigan where he'd watched her put her folded resignation as they'd walked to her apartment building. She stared at him, startled, as he retrieved it.

"You're back on the team, aren't you, Sheely?" Trey held the small folded square of paper in his hand.

The elevator lurched to a stop and the doors swung open.

"I'm here, aren't I?" Callie murmured. "I guess that means I am back on the team."

Was that the purpose of last night? she wondered, and another seed of anxiety took root within her. Had Trey gone to bed with her strictly to induce her to discard her resignation?

Seduce to induce. The words clanged in her head like a bad imitation of Dr. Seuss.

"Good." Trey ripped up the paper into confetti-size pieces and tossed them into a trash bin they passed. "Sheely, I'd like a promise that you won't pull that stunt again."

"I'm not in the habit of making promises I can't keep," Callie replied, and quickly entered the women's locker room to grab a scrub suit.

This time Trey didn't come charging in after her.

Seven

She didn't see him again until both had scrubbed and donned their masks, caps and gowns before entering one of the Children's Hospital operating rooms.

It was already noisy and crowded inside, the sense of emergency pervasive, even a bit desperate.

"Trey Weldon here," Trey announced, and someone immediately called him over to the operating table where the Hagen boy lay anesthetized, surrounded by a plethora of surgeons working on every part of his injured body.

Callie saw the team of OR nurses already busy at work, knew that her presence at the table would be superfluous and quietly took a place against the far wall.

Working in tandem with the pediatric neurosurgeon, Trey successfully curbed the intracranial bleeding, but every other vital organ in the patient's body also had suffered dangerous injuries, requiring the attention of every specialist summoned.

By the time the patient was wheeled out of the OR and

into the trauma intensive care unit hours later, everybody, from the surgical team to the crowd of onlookers, was drained from the series of near catastrophes.

"The kid will never last the morning. He'll probably go out in Recovery." Callie overheard one surgeon say to another.

"Ahh, man, look at the time! Almost eight o'clock," one of the doctors moaned, as they filed out of the OR. Callie was among the last to leave. The VIPs, like Trey departed first.

Callie tossed her cap and mask and gown into the bin provided. She had to be in the Tri-State OR in about fifteen minutes, just enough time to take a quick shower over there and change into fresh scrubs.

Trey suddenly appeared in front of her.

"Trey, what you did in there was incredible," she told him admiringly, because it was true.

The pediatric neurosurgeon specializing in trauma had not only requested Trey's assistance in stemming the boy's subarachnoid hemorrhage but praised his inventive emergency technique to the assembled crowd of professionals.

"We got the boy off the table alive," Trey interrupted flatly. "I've never seen any patient with so many injuries to so many vital organs. But that doesn't stop our colleagues from debating their bad-seed theory, does it?" His voice grew harsh, and his blue eyes were cold and hard.

"I don't know what you're talking about." Callie was confused. "What bad-seed theory?"

"How could you not hear about it? There was a constant buzz going on in the OR and in the locker room afterward about how Hagen's kid has been in trouble almost since he learned to walk. A few wondered why we were working so hard to patch up a kid who's going to end up in prison. His grandfather, an ex-con with apparently no redeeming virtue, was mentioned as the genetic source of trouble."

"People actually questioned treating this boy because

they think he might have prison in his future if he lives?'' Callie exclaimed, appalled. ''As for the criminal grandfather, well, the curse of bad blood is practically a horror novel cliché, isn't it? You know, tired old genre fiction.''

''Not tired enough, apparently. It seems that even Paul Hagen himself has shared concern about his son's genetic makeup with enough people that it's common knowledge. Of course, the family criminal isn't one of the Hagens.''

''So the maternal grandfather is the baddie?''

''You aren't taking this very seriously.'' Abruptly he changed gears. ''Don't forget, we're removing a pituitary tumor at eight-fifteen,'' he said brusquely. ''Mrs. Knezovic in OR three. We have to get over to Tri-State immediately.''

''I'm on my way there now,'' she replied.

He wasn't there to hear. There was a labyrinth of tunnels inter-connecting the five hospitals, and Trey was already heading toward the passage with signs directing pedestrians to the Tri-State Medical Center.

Callie followed him. After all, she had no choice; they were going to the same place. She thought of her resignation, in pieces in a trash can.

What if she had refused to disregard it? Would he still be making an effort to persuade her to rejoin his surgical team? *Don't pull this stunt again,* he'd ordered. As if she had been playacting in a bid for his attention!

Well, she'd gotten attention from him, all right, Callie acknowledged grimly. And if Trey's sole objective in making love to her was to regain her services as his chief scrub nurse, did that mean their brief time together as lovers was over since he'd achieved his goal?

In addition to all her other firsts last night, should she add ''first one-night stand'' to the list? Callie flinched at that painful thought.

She trudged along, her eyes to the ground, the distressing thoughts bouncing around in her head.

Though their lovemaking had taken place hours earlier,

she could still feel the effects of it. She was sore in certain intimate places, and there was physical evidence of him on her, within her. Paradoxically, those very signs of their intimacy seemed to accentuate the distance between them now, a distance that was both literal and figurative.

Callie tried to work up some righteous anger, but she had neither the heart or the energy for it. All she felt was sadness, mixed with emptiness and exhaustion.

"If you walk any slower, you'll be going backward." Trey's voice rang out, echoing a little in the tunnel.

She jerked her head up to see him about a hundred yards ahead of her. He had come to an abrupt halt.

"If I walk any faster, I'll collapse," she muttered, though she knew he couldn't hear her from where he was standing.

She fully expected him to resume his speed-of-light pace, but he remained where he was, his arms folded in front of his chest, watching her.

Waiting for her?

Callie didn't kid herself about that or even dare to hope. But she forced herself to quicken her stride. Her legs were aching, and she was panting when she finally reached him.

"It's about time." Trey gazed down at her as she came to stand beside him.

"I was going as fast as I could." Callie was defensive. And out of breath. "It's not like I was deliberately lollygagging, you know."

"Lollygagging," he repeated. "Good choice of words, because that's exactly what you were doing. And there's no time for it. Let's go." He started off again at an even faster pace.

Still breathless, her muscles protesting, Callie could only resume her earlier slower pace.

Trey stopped, frowning, when he realized that she'd dropped behind him again. "If this is some passive-aggressive game you're playing, Callie, I—"

"I'm too tired to play games," she retorted. "I've been

on my feet for hours after very little sleep..." She blushed and immediately fell silent, remembering why she hadn't slept much.

"I could use the same excuse, couldn't I?" Trey looked rather smug. "And up the ante because *I* was operating while you were merely standing."

"Sorry, but I'm not bionic like you are. Most of us mortals aren't. I can't keep up with you. I freely admit it."

"Try," he ordered. "I want us to be in the OR a couple of minutes before the patient is brought in."

"I'll be there exactly at eight-fifteen, no earlier, unless you want me to ride piggyback," Callie snapped, tiring of the entire issue. "On *your* back," she added pointedly. The mere suggestion of such a public spectacle should instantly send the proper Dr. Weldon on his way, leaving her to walk to her destination in peace.

But Trey stayed right where he was. "All right. Get on."

Her jaw dropped. It now seemed that her lack of sleep was wreaking havoc on her mental processes as well as her physical stamina, because she could've sworn he said...

"Put your arms around my neck, and I'll boost you up." Trey turned his back to her and leaned over slightly, presumably so she could reach her arms around his neck.

Callie stood motionless. "I...you...we can't," she stammered.

"Who says we can't?" he demanded.

Wrong choice of words, she realized. People like Trey Weldon weren't used to hearing the word *can't*. It didn't apply to them.

"We'd better not," she corrected weakly.

"Why not? It makes perfect sense. We'll get to the OR early. Now hop up."

"We made it with plenty of time to spare, just as I said we would," Trey announced, setting Callie on her feet in front of Tri-State's women's surgical locker room. "I'll see you in the OR in approximately eight minutes."

He immediately ducked into the men's locker room, pulled off one set of scrubs and headed for the showers.

Five minutes later he had showered, dried and was wearing a fresh scrub suit as he began to lather his hands with the antibacterial soap provided at the sink right outside the operating room.

The automatic, methodical handwashing provided an opportunity for his mind to drift. *What a night!*

Immediately Trey's heart began to race. He realized he was glad of the hectic pace this morning; with the two surgeries almost back-to-back, he'd scarcely had a spare moment to stop and think.

And that was a good thing, because thinking about last night's passion—before, during and after—was the last thing he wanted to do.

Yet the thoughts he had been able to suppress so easily during the Hagen boy's emergency surgery now flooded him like a river overflowing its dam.

It was unnerving that his feelings for Callie were so overwhelming. They overpowered him in a way he'd never experienced before. And since he didn't know what to do about that, at least he didn't want to have to think about it.

But his usual practice of compartmentalizing was not working. How could he *not* think about last night?

Last night he had given in and let his feelings, his desire and need, dictate his actions. Before his mind's eye flashed images of himself tracking down Callie, going to that dump and dragging her out of it, taking her home.

And to bed...

All impulsive acts by a man who did not act on impulse, who had trained himself to stay in control at all times. Well, he hadn't been in control last night.

His uncharacteristic behavior hadn't been limited to last night either, Trey reminded himself—as if he could ever forget! Carrying Callie piggyback through the tunnel this morning was another extremely unWeldon-like act.

He'd enjoyed it, too, all of it. The seductive feel of her legs wrapped around his waist, her arms around his neck. The softness of her breasts nestled against his back, even her small, embarrassed moans at the smiles and jocular remarks directed to them by passersby.

Trey actually smiled. That little piggyback ride had revived all of last night's erotic memories and the warmly affectionate ones, too. Of holding her, having her close. Feeling her so near, as if she were part of him.

He had never been possessive before—well, perhaps only of the Weldon name and its traditions—but certainly never about a woman. But he definitely felt possessive toward Callie, and he didn't even try to pretend otherwise to himself.

What was he going to do about it? About her? He had broken some major rules, and one thing he had learned very early was that there were consequences to every action. Consequences...

"You're going to take your skin off if you scrub any harder, Doc," joked Leo Arkis, who'd arrived and stood beside Trey, eyeing him speculatively.

Leo appeared well rested and annoyingly chipper. Trey scowled at him.

"I spent hours last night in surgery. An emergency involving Paul Hagen's boy," Trey stated stolidly. "Tough case." He went on scrubbing his already sterile skin and proceeded to give Leo a brief summary of the accident and its aftermath.

Callie and Quiana were already in the OR when Trey and Leo entered. There wasn't a big crowd of observers today, though some med students and nursing students were there, along with the neurosurgery resident. This wasn't a ground-breaking operation. Pituitary tumors were fairly common and rarely complicated.

"I always tell patients who have a pituitary tumor, 'If you

have to have a tumor in your head, you picked the right one.'" Trey began his usual speech for this operation. He wasn't on automatic pilot, but somewhat close to it.

His eyes met Callie's as she handed him the instrument he needed before he had to ask. She knew this minilecture of his so well that she could predict what action he would take during which particular sentence.

Their professional rapport hadn't been adversely affected by their sexual escapades of last night, and Trey was greatly, silently relieved. He didn't realize how much he had been dreading the possibility that their affinity in the OR might have been ruined by sex.

But it wasn't. He and Callie were working together as intuitively, as smoothly, as ever.

After the harrowing touch-and-go surgery on the Hagen boy, this morning's operation with Callie and his team and his favorite tumor was actually restorative. Trey felt his energy level rise. He wielded his instrument with expert precision, he answered questions and added memorable details to enhance the students' learning experience.

"Dr. Weldon, if you ever decide not to operate anymore, you would make a fantastic anatomy teacher," one of the female medical students said to him after the operation was over and the patient had been taken to recovery.

The med student had approached him just outside the OR. "I feel I learned more about the skull and the brain in here today than during a whole semester in anatomy class," she added, vivacious and enthusiastic.

"Thank you. And I won't say a word about that to Cy Nichols." Trey grinned as he mentioned the medical school's anatomy professor.

The student laughed appreciatively.

Callie watched the exchange from a few feet away.

"*Et tu*, Dr. Weldon?" murmured Quiana, who was standing with Callie and also watching.

Quiana did not bother to disguise her disapproval. "Is

Trey flirting with that med student? Just because she's pretty and looking at him as though he's a big rich dessert! Geez, I always thought he was above responding to that kind of behavior. I was proud that he was.''

Callie pulled off her surgical cap and ran her hand through her hair, still wet from her speedy shower. She'd managed to get it washed, but there was no time for drying it. She suspected her ponytail more closely resembled a drowned rat's tail.

Worse, she had on no underwear beneath her oversize scrubs because she couldn't bear the thought of putting back on last night's unfresh panties and bra after showering. Bad enough that she'd had to wear them through the predawn surgery, but Trey had rushed her out of her apartment so fast she'd had no time even to reach into her drawer for clean lingerie.

Her cheeks flushed scarlet as provocative memories assailed her. Of how she'd awakened naked in his arms, how he'd helped dress her…after undressing her last night.

In the midst of her erotic reverie, her beeper sounded, much to her surprise. Since Trey was still deep in conversation with the med student—whose glowing eyes never left his face—who could be paging her?

A quick phone call later, she knew. She was to report to the director of nursing's office immediately. Not surprisingly, Ellen McCann wanted to talk about her hasty resignation yesterday. Nor did the director intend to let Trey's visit and his insistence upon taking the signed resignation go unmentioned.

"Since you're back at work on Trey Weldon's surgical team, I assume your resignation is no longer valid, Ms. Sheely?" The older woman studied Callie intently.

"Yes." Callie nodded her head. "And I apologize for my—for acting so irrationally yesterday. I would like to forget the resignation incident ever happened."

"Obviously, so would Trey Weldon. Callie, you're an excellent nurse. I hope you know how much you are valued here at Tri-State. Because you certainly are.''

''Thank you, Mrs. McCann.''

The director took a deep breath. ''I would like you to be completely honest with me, Callie. Did Trey Weldon threaten or coerce you into reconsidering your resignation?''

''Threaten or coerce?'' Callie repeated and thought of her earlier painful musings. *Seduce to induce.* But she wasn't about to share that with the director of nursing!

''I promise that it's safe for you to tell me the truth,'' Ellen McCann assured her. ''If there is sexual harassment going on, which prompted you to quit in the first place, I want it reported so action can be taken immediately. I will not tolerate any of my nurses enduring any kind of abuse from *anyone,* no matter how exalted their position in this hospital.''

Callie winced. ''Oh, no, it's nothing like that!''

Hearing aspersions, especially false ones, cast on Trey was viscerally painful for her. Seduction didn't really apply, Callie decided. She had been a more than willing participant. If she hadn't been in love with Trey, she would have told him to get lost without a moment's hesitation.

''I...I overreacted yesterday, Mrs. McCann. Trey would never harass or abuse anyone.'' Callie realized she was blushing. Had she ever been so mortified in her life?

''I want you to know that I am documenting the meetings dealing with your resignation and its withdrawal, as well as the one I had with Trey Weldon,'' Ellen McCann continued. ''Not only for the hospital's legal protection but for your own, Callie.''

This time Callie cringed. ''I understand, but I don't need protection from Trey, Mrs. McCann. Truly.'' Reflexively she rose to her feet, literally emphasizing her stand on the matter. And hopefully bringing this excruciating meeting to a close.

Ellen McCann took the cue and rose, too. She walked

Callie to the door, laying a hand on her arm to delay her momentary departure.

"I have daughters, you know. And I feel I can't let you leave without asking you this question. Have you carefully thought out what you're doing, Callie? Becoming, er, involved with someone you work with closely can be—" she paused "—detrimental in a number of ways."

"Thank you for your understanding, Mrs. McCann," Callie said, because she had no answer to her supervisor's question.

Of course she hadn't thought out her involvement with Trey! It had suddenly escalated, exploding into passion last night. *No, she couldn't think about that now, especially not here!*

Callie said a quick goodbye and tried to make a hasty exit. But Ellen McCann was leaving the office herself and walked with Callie through her secretary's small reception area and into the corridor.

Both women stopped in their tracks at the sight of Trey Weldon, leaning against the wall a few feet from the director's office suite. Callie stole a quick glance at Ellen McCann. The nursing director's eyebrows were raised so high they looked like the McDonald's arches.

"Hello," Trey greeted them casually as he ambled to meet them.

Callie knew his seemingly nonchalant tone and stroll was anything but.

"The Hagen boy is holding his own over at Children's," Trey told Mrs. McCann, though she hadn't asked. "It's a good sign. However, his prognosis remains extremely guarded."

"I'm sure everyone's prayers and good wishes go out to the Hagens at this difficult time," Ellen replied smoothly. She turned completely away from him to direct a laser-sharp gaze at Callie. "I want you to think about what we discussed, Callie. Will you do that?"

Callie nodded, feeling completely out of her element, keeping her eyes averted from Trey. She sensed, she *knew*, his were not averted from her, though. She could feel his burning gaze touching her.

The couple stood in silence as Mrs. McCann glided down the corridor, away from them.

"She's mastered the subtle art of intimidation, I'll give her that," said Trey, as the director turned a corner and went out of sight.

Callie realized she'd been holding her breath and took in a gulp of air. "She's documenting the meetings about…my resignation—the two she had with me and the one with you."

Despite the embarrassment, she felt obliged to divulge the information. She expected him to be livid about this smudge on his impeccable professional reputation.

"Is that why she wanted to see you?" Trey seemed to take the news calmly enough. "To tell you that?"

"And to ask if I know what I'm doing." Callie started walking. "Because she doesn't think I do."

"Surely she doesn't mean that in the professional sense." Trey fell into step alongside her. "You're one of the best operating room nurses in the entire area, Sheely."

Sheely! His use of her surname, which had never bothered her, which she'd even liked until this morning, now affected her like a glass of ice water thrown in her face. She hated how it made her feel.

His shoulder brushed hers as they walked. Had she imagined his elbow grazing her breast? Callie moved away from him, till she was practically hugging the wall.

"Mrs. McCann also wanted to know if you were harassing or abusing me in any way." She knew she was taking too much pleasure informing him of *that*.

"Well, am I?" Trey was right beside her again, then moved in front of her, trapping her between the wall and himself.

Callie felt the heat radiating from his body, only an inch or two from hers. "I wonder if pinning me against the wall would qualify as harassment?" she asked flippantly.

She felt light-headed. The lack of sleep, the professional demands of the past hours, the aftermath of the Trey-induced emotional intensity, all might have contributed to her condition.

But being so close to the irresistible fire and strength of his body was undoubtedly the catalyst that provoked her next action.

She needed to do *something* physical, but she was too uncertain of him to do what she would like to do—grasp him and kiss him senseless. Instead, right there in the corridor, at the moment fortunately deserted, she raised her hands to push him away.

Trey's lightning-fast reflexes superceded her attempt. He caught both her wrists with one hand and held them between their bodies. "I want an answer, Callie."

She felt his knuckles brush her breasts, and the tips instantly tightened. That she could be so swiftly aroused by such a small gesture infuriated her.

It wasn't fair! He need only *look* at her to send her head spinning, while he remained cool and in command, of himself and of her.

"You're so upset about a possible mar on your flawless reputation that you hightailed it down here the minute Quiana told you Ellen had called to see me." Callie fairly spit out the words.

Whatever his motives were last night, she was not going to allow herself to be so easily seduced today. "Oh, yes, I know exactly how and why you're here." She said sharply, mostly to remind herself. She tried to pull her wrists away.

"Do you?" His grip was like iron and he wouldn't let her go.

"Yes. You guessed Mrs. McCann was going to discuss the resignation business with me and you just *had* to check out the situation. So you tore yourself away from your…your *hungry* med student and—''

''Oh, please! Don't bother to pretend you were jealous of any student, Callie. You know that I—that you—'' Unable not to, he moved in even closer to her, letting her feel the hard heat of his erection.

''We have to talk,'' he said hoarsely. ''Now.''

Later, Callie would wonder if it was sheer fate or if Trey had known all along that the door to a utility room was just a few feet away from them, therefore choosing that particular place to confront her.

Whatever. Within seconds he'd yanked open the door and pulled her inside, closing the door behind them. She heard the lock click shut.

Eight

The sudden plunge into total darkness was disorienting. Callie blinked her eyes. It made no difference whether they were open or closed, there was only the surrounding blackness.

The rest of her senses took over, going into hyperdrive to compensate for her lack of sight. Or maybe it was her fierce desire for him, her deep love for him, that was responsible for the flood of sensual awareness engulfing her.

He'd released her wrists when he closed the door, and Callie used her freedom to lay her hands on his chest, to glide them down to his waist. She could feel him, smell him, hear his rapid breathing.

"I came down here for one reason only," he rasped, pressing his mouth against the side of her neck, gently kissing and nipping. "To see you. I wanted to talk to you after surgery, but you ran off—"

"I was paged and you were busy," Callie corrected.

She arched her neck, allowing him greater access and

leaned into him, relaxing fully against him. She was achingly aware of his strength and her need for him; she was overwhelmed by it, turned on by it.

"You never did say if I am harassing or abusing you." His lips brushed her ear, the tip of his tongue exploring the delicate shell shape. "Am I?"

"No, never." She moaned softly.

Even in the darkness his mouth unerringly found hers, and he brushed his lips slowly back and forth over hers. "Kiss me," he whispered to her.

She pressed her lips against his, exerting a gentle pressure. At the same moment she slid her arms around his neck to bring herself even closer to him.

They both sighed at the satisfying contact.

His mouth took hers, his tongue sliding between her parted lips, and he kissed her deeply. She responded passionately, slipping her own tongue into the tantalizing heat of his mouth to explore, to taste him.

His hands moved over her, tracing her soft curves, and she writhed against him, encouraging his caresses to become bolder. He slid his hands under her big, loose-fitting scrub shirt and found her breasts, free of a bra. With a groan of pleasure, he cupped them, fondling the rounded softness, his thumbs circling the already taut, sensitive crests.

Callie trembled with arousal. His caresses, his kisses were wildly exciting and for a few moments she simply relished the exquisite pleasure of it all.

But soon it wasn't enough to remain passive, to be only on the receiving end of this sensual bliss. She wanted to give and give to him, to share the pleasure and their passion.

She wanted what they'd had last night, a consummation of their mutual desire, the full expression of their love.

Her hands moved restlessly over him, then became more purposeful as she stroked the damp, bare skin of his back under his scrub shirt. Her fingers kneaded the muscled smoothness, savoring the feel of him.

"I want you, I want you." His voice was deep and low and sexy, resonating with urgency and desire. "It's never been like this for me before."

She had always been entranced by the well-modulated masculine timbre of his voice, but never more than now. His words, his tone, sent her soaring.

Boldly she dipped her hands beneath the elastic waistband of his scrub pants.

As usual, they were in perfect sync with each other, mutually attuned in thought and action. Because at that same moment, his big hands slid under her scrubs to touch the cool, soft skin of her bottom.

Simultaneously they discovered that neither was wearing any underwear.

"It's like a fantasy," Trey groaned, slipping his hands between her legs to find her hot center.

"Yes," Callie agreed dizzily.

It was exactly like one of the many, many fantasies she'd had about the two of them, and the cloak of darkness only added to the dreamlike aura.

He cupped her, his fingers parting her, teasing and exciting her as she moaned into his mouth.

"You're so wet, so ready for me," Trey rasped. "Let me, Callie. Please."

Her slender fingers grasped him. It was thrilling to know she could affect him like this. His masculinity made her feel ultrafeminine, empowering her by his need for her.

She felt him push her scrub pants down and tugged at his. He helped her, quickly divesting himself and her of the annoying impediments.

She could feel the remaining vestiges of his control snap and knew he couldn't wait another moment. Neither could she. Relinquishing her own control was a sweet relief, a pleasure in itself.

His big hands curved around her buttocks, and he lifted

her up against the heavy door. Reflexively she wrapped her legs around him, her hands clutching his shoulders.

With one firm thrust he was inside her, filling her. Callie cried out, and he stopped. But before he could say anything, she'd opened her legs wider, and her hands were pushing at his hips, urging him deeper.

Their mouths were fused, as well, their tongues, their lips moving in exciting, excruciating simulation.

They moved eagerly together, wild rhythms matching, sensual urgency and heat building to flashpoint. Simultaneously, their passion erupted into an explosive climax, hurling them both into the sweet mindless realm of rapture.

Trey collapsed against the door, still holding her, their bodies still joined. He buried his face in the hollow of her shoulder as she lay her head on his shoulder.

Callie was filled with peace and sighed a soft, contented sigh. She sensed that the intimacy of their mutual release had dissolved all barriers between them. She felt closer to him than she'd ever felt to anyone.

"Even though I'm back on the team," she murmured a little dazedly, "you still want me."

"To quote you to yourself… 'Duh!'" Trey laughed at his own joke.

Though it was goofy, Callie laughed, too.

A goofy Trey Weldon was most unusual. And so appealing. Sheer happiness mushroomed inside her. They remained silently, blissfully locked together for a few more moments.

Finally Callie raised her head slightly and looked around. "There's enough light coming in under the door that I think my eyes are finally starting to adjust a little to the dark."

"Just don't tell me you see Ellen McCann over there in the corner, documenting us," Trey said drolly.

Callie gave an appreciative chuckle. "Not to worry, we're alone. I see a big sink over there and I think I can make out the outline of the floor-waxing machine and some brooms and mops and buckets."

She sighed again and laid her head back down on his shoulder. "Such a romantic setting. Who needs soft music and candlelight?"

"Not to mention a bed."

Callie smiled in the darkness. "Who needs one of those?"

"Callie, I have to confess, I've never done this before. In all the hospitals I've worked in during medical school, my residencies, my tenure here, I've never made love in a utility room."

"Well, I don't make a practice of it, either," she teased, gently rubbing his jaw with the tip of her nose.

He managed to catch her lips for a kiss that left her breathless.

"The effect you have on me is... I can't find the word...." His voice trailed off in a mumble.

She wondered if she ought to help him out and supply one. Like *love*.

Callie tightened her grip on him. It was time to tell him the truth. The closeness and tenderness between them made it easy. And as soon as she told him about her virginity, she would tell him that she was in love with him.

"Trey, when I said I don't make a practice of making love in utility rooms, I—well, it's not just utility rooms where I've remained, um, chaste. I've—"

"Never made love during working hours or at the hospital?" Trey guessed, interrupting. "Truth to tell, neither have I, Callie. I've always been too busy, too tired, too professional, too something, I guess. Except today I'm busy, tired and the rest, but it didn't seem to matter."

Callie's heart leaped joyfully. He was skirting very close to revealing that she was someone very special to him. And wasn't that close enough to telling her that he loved her?

It was definitely time to share her secret with him, to tell him she loved him.

"Trey, last night—" Her voice quavered with emotion. She breathed deeply and tried again. "Last night was the first time I've ever made love anywhere with anybody. I'm so glad it was with you.''

The following silence stretched beyond any comfortable, shared intimacy. Trey was so silent and so still that if their bodies hadn't still been joined, if every inch of her hadn't been touching him, she might've thought he was no longer there.

She couldn't even hear him breathing. Had he stopped?

''Trey?'' Her voice rose nervously.

''Let me be certain I heard this correctly. You were a virgin until last night.'' His voice held the same clinical detachment as when he was describing the difference between anaplastic and pleomorphic astrocytomas to a group assembled in the OR.

''Yes,'' Callie whispered. What did he...? Why was he...?

''Is it true, or are you just saying it because you think it might be something I want to hear?''

Callie went cold. Happiness and contentment fled, and suddenly she was painfully, terribly aware of the tawdriness of this situation. *They had ducked into a utility room and had sex!*

It was an outrageous act, completely out of character for her, for him, for anyone except the heroes, heroines and villains starring on daytime television—and at least *their* trysts were scripted.

This one certainly wasn't.

She immediately unwrapped her limbs from around him, sliding to the ground on legs that felt weak and shaky. ''From your tone it doesn't sound as though it was something you wanted to hear.'' Callie stooped down, fumbling on the ground for her scrub pants. When she found them, she pulled them on.

''And if you think I would make up something like that to...to...what, Trey? Why would you think I'd do it? To impress you? To manipulate you? I've never been so insulted in my whole life!''

''I didn't mean to insult you.'' But his tone held no hint of apology. ''But if it's true—''

''It is!'' She tried to get to the lock, but he was standing in front of the door. ''Let me out right now!''

''So you can run to the director of nursing and quit again?''

She heard the rustle of cloth and could dimly discern him readjusting his scrub pants. She was grateful that the darkness made it impossible for her to see his expression. Simply imagining his frown of disapproval, his cold stare, was bad enough.

Furthermore, she would rather drown in the big sink in the corner than to have Trey see the tears in her eyes. She would never let him see her cry, especially not over him!

''I don't like to repeat myself, so no, I won't quit,'' she snapped, anger bolstering her. ''You'll have to fire me this time.''

''Now you're getting hysterical. What I—''

''If you think this is hysterical, you haven't seen hysteria,'' Callie said cutting in.

She certainly had. Bonnie was the preeminent drama queen when displeased. Right about now, Bonnie would probably be screaming the door down while whacking Trey with the nearest available weapon—a mop, no doubt.

''I'm hungry. I want to get some lunch before our next surgery.'' Callie did her best to sound calm and rational. Which wasn't easy, as she felt far from either.

But she had to get them back on safe ground, professional ground, to put this awful scene behind them. ''It's the giant intracranial aneurysm on Peter Sorkin.''

''The advertising executive.'' Trey nodded, immediately reviewing the facts of the case. ''It's a giant aneurysm, all right, two point seven centimeters in diameter. Luckily for him, we've successfully repaired even larger ones.''

"Yes, we have," agreed Callie.

For those brief moments everything seemed normal between them. Perhaps Trey thought it was. But when he placed his hands on Callie's forearms, she went rigid. "Don't touch me."

He dropped his hands immediately. "Callie, we can't dodge this. What you haven't let me say is why your, er, declaration of virginity is of such grave concern to me," he added stiffly.

Callie considered making some caustic comeback to *declaration of virginity,* a phrase that certainly inspired sarcasm. But she restrained herself.

Either encouraged or uncomfortable with her silence, Trey took a deep breath and continued.

"Not that I gave it a single thought at the time but—last night I used no form of birth control." He didn't sound clinically detached now. He sounded as if he were in deep despair. "When I did think about it today, I assumed that since you hadn't mentioned anything last night, you were protected. On the Pill or something."

"Sorry." Callie was flip. "Last night *I* didn't give it a single thought, either. In fact, I didn't think about protection until right this minute, which shows you just how *backward* I really am in the...the sexual arena."

"No, you mustn't think that. What happened last night—and today—is all my fault." Trey groaned. "Twice, I didn't think before I acted. *Twice!* That kind of impulsiveness is unforgivable. A sign of a serious character flaw."

Callie heaved a sigh. She was furious with him, she was hurt, but he sounded so distraught. *A serious character flaw?* He was exhibiting more remorse for lapsing into passion than some killers on Death Row for all their evil crimes!

She felt a twinge of sympathy for him. Dr. Trey Weldon was the man who never made mistakes, and now he'd just faced the appalling truth that he'd erred *twice.* He found it so upsetting that he was ready to label himself as having a personality disorder.

Poor Trey. Callie smiled grimly. Was there a self-help book offering consolation and advice to perfect people who'd just realized that they couldn't be perfect all the time? Trey certainly seemed to be in need of one.

She was unable to watch him torture himself any longer. "Trey, it's hardly a capital offense. We both—"

"Don't make excuses for me, Callie. You are sexually inexperienced, and it was my responsibility to protect us both. I didn't. I can assure you that you're under no threat of catching any disease, because in the past I've always been scrupulously careful. But as for the other risk—pregnancy—" He fairly gasped the word.

"You don't have to worry about that. It's the wrong time," she said quickly. "My period is due today or tomorrow."

Callie was surprised she wasn't blushing. A day ago discussing such intimacies with Trey would've turned every inch of her skin beet-red. Not now.

"Hey, I know! I'll pin the blame for my wild behavior on PMS. People are always claiming raging hormones make them do crazy things. Women have beaten homicide raps with the PMS defense, so it's certainly legit to use for two scenes of unbridled, unprotected sex. You can use it, too. Just say I raped you."

"That isn't funny," growled Trey. "You sound coarse and hard and bratty and...and—"

"Lower-class?" Callie suggested. "Well, I am from a lower class than you are, Trey. In fact, so are most people. All those exclusive organizations for the upper class wouldn't be so exclusive if the majority of the population were eligible to join."

"Don't try to turn this around into something else, Callie. If you're pregnant—"

"I'm not."

"If you're pregnant," he continued, as if she hadn't interrupted, "I'll do the right thing, of course."

"I see. And that would be?"

"Stop this," he snapped. "Stop it right now. You know that I'll marry you if you're pregnant. I have spent my whole life acting responsibly, making sure that I am a credit to the Weldon name, and I don't intend to change now. Even though—"

"Even though the thought of marrying me makes you nauseous?" Callie completed the rest of his sentence. "Well, I—"

"Don't put words into my mouth," Trey snapped. "If you'd given me a chance to finish, you would have heard me say I didn't plan to marry anyone until I'm forty. *Anyone,* Callie," he added emphatically.

"Forty?" Callie repeated, nonplussed. "*Forty?* My dad and mom are both forty-six. All their kids are adults, but at their same age, yours wouldn't even be in school yet. Unless you don't want children at all?"

She asked the question in the same tone she would use to ask him if he didn't want to use anesthesia for a patient during surgery. Horrified and uncomprehending.

Trey frowned. "Yes, I'd like to have a child or two. But no earlier than I've planned."

"And at what age would that be?" Callie prodded caustically. "Fifty? Sixty? You don't want to rush into anything, do you?"

"Forty is a good age to marry," Trey replied, his expression glacial. "My brother married at forty, and he and his wife now have a two-year-old son, Winston III. We call him Little Chip, and he's a wonderful child. Win's done everything just right, as usual."

"Well, so have you. Don't even *try* to claim to be the Weldon family screwup, it just won't wash."

And if he actually believed such a preposterous notion, it only went to show how frighteningly high the Weldons set their standards. Which reinforced her belief that she could never be considered proper Weldon material.

Callie bristled defensively. "Believe it or not, I've spent my whole life acting responsibly, too, except for... what happened with you. *Twice!* And maybe I should thank you for your... your noble offer of marriage if need be, but no thanks. No matter what, I won't punish myself by marrying a man who can only view me as a miserable duty, as a creature way beneath his worth."

She reached around him, groping on the wall for the light switch, then flicked it on. She caught a quick glimpse of Trey squinting against the flood of light and used his moment of distraction to her advantage.

"I'll see you in the OR in about an hour," she announced, quickly unlocking the door. Just as fast, she was out of the utility closet and into the corridor.

This time it wasn't deserted. Medical personnel walked alone or in groups, luckily too caught up in their own thoughts or conversations to give her a glance as she strode swiftly down the hall.

She had enough of an advance on Trey that he couldn't have caught up with her without running, which she knew he would not do. Such behavior was too uncivilized for the properly decorous Dr. Weldon.

Their piggyback ride through the tunnel, hardly proper or decorous, flashed to mind, but she dismissed the incident as an aberration, probably the result of his lack of sleep, or possibly the adrenaline high of emergency surgery.

Obviously, he'd regained his balance and his Weldon dignity. She knew he had, because he didn't even *try* to pursue her.

Callie told herself she was glad. It was time to face facts. Her brief fling with Trey Weldon was over, and though it hurt, she wasn't going to repeat her stupid emotional behavior of yesterday. Today there would be no race to Ellen McCann's office, no resignation.

She and Trey would go back to being colleagues, period. After all, their professional relationship worked. They wonderfully complemented each other in the operating room, a fact proven countless times.

Their intimate relationship as lovers hadn't fared so well. They'd been impulsive and reckless, not their usual calm, sensible, responsible selves. Most important, there was no future in a personal relationship with Trey, even if she were Weldon bride material, because she couldn't passively wile away seven years of her life waiting for him to reach his designated age of marriage.

She had no doubt that if Trey Weldon decided that he would marry at forty, he would—and not a day earlier.

Could they ever go back to what they'd been, or had sex, and the whole range of emotions flowing from it, ruined the perfect working relationship? Callie wondered...and worried.

Her anxiety lifted later that day in the OR, when she and Trey automatically resumed their familiar professional roles. The two of them worked together in perfect harmony, their unspoken communication fluent and effortless.

It was such a stunning contrast to the awkward conversation they'd tried to have after sex in the utility room. Yes, keeping their relationship platonic and professional was a wise decision, the most rational, practical course of action.

If only she didn't want so much more with him, if only she didn't love him so much!

But that was *her* problem, because Trey seemed to have no trouble forgetting what had happened between them.

The next three days were like all the days preceding those bouts of tempestuous lovemaking. Callie and Trey worked smoothly together in the OR, but there was no private contact between them away from it.

In the lounge between surgeries, they were surrounded by others, Leo and Quiana and the usual assortment of operating room personnel: nurses, surgeons, anesthesiologists and the rest. Callie didn't have a moment alone with Trey, and in the presence of their colleagues the two of them didn't exchange a single word that could be construed as mildly personal.

However, there was one major difference between what Callie secretly termed pre-and postpassion. Trey never touched her anymore.

Prepassion, he had done so naturally and often. It had been a delicious form of torture, one she longed for now, his casual hand on her back, her shoulder, her arm. Anywhere!

But Trey didn't come near her. It was as though she were radioactive, and direct contact with her would contaminate him. Maybe he did feel contaminated by her, Callie speculated gloomily, but not in a nuclear way. In a social way.

She'd fallen so hard for him that she had forgotten an important rule. In Trey's world, wealthy upper-class blue bloods didn't consort with working-class peons. And if they happened to slip and *consort* a time or two, discretion ruled, and it was never mentioned again.

So Callie followed his lead and pretended she and Trey had never made love, that she didn't know how he felt buried deep and full inside her, that she hadn't run her hands over his bare skin, touching him, learning the pleasure of his hard male body.

She pretended that he was simply a doctor she worked with and that he hadn't been her first lover, who'd brought her to complete satisfaction. She pretended she wasn't in love with him and she didn't ache for his touch.

It wasn't easy, but Callie kept up the pretense, her acting skills never faltering.

She was such an excellent actress that Trey was completely fooled by her performance. Every day at the hospital he saw the calm, competent and unemotional Nurse Sheely, who was completely absorbed in her work and completely uninterested in him.

Sometimes he found himself wondering if he had dreamed that night in her bed and their wild little interlude in the utility closet, because for the past three days Callie was so aloof and so very cool...well, icy as a glacier would be more accurate.

She didn't look at him, she looked through him, as if he weren't there. Her beautiful brown eyes, which had shone with passion during that night they'd spent together, which had been filled with laughter or flamed with anger during conversations they'd had in those days before they'd made love, now viewed him with dispassionate detachment.

Now there was no conversation between the two of them. People around them chatted—there were *always* people around—but Callie didn't direct a word in his direction. She spoke to him in the OR if need be; if he asked her a direct question, she replied, but only in the most impersonal manner.

Trey couldn't help but notice how she made a special effort to maintain distance between them. Literally. He knew all about the concept of personal space, but Callie was carrying it to extremes. He got the feeling she'd prefer to have the personal space between her and him as wide as the continent of Asia.

Adding to his frustration, and sometimes his relief, they were never ever alone. Callie herself saw to that, fastening herself to somebody's—anybody's!—side if he tried to approach her.

The occasional meals they'd shared in the hospital cafeteria were a thing of the past. These days she was always seated between two people, usually at a table that was already full. Too often, Jimmy Dimarino was with her, and Trey was quick to observe that there was no distance, literal or figurative, between that pair.

No, cold, competent Nurse Sheely was nothing like Callie, the passionate woman who all too briefly had been his lover.

After endlessly ruminating on how badly he had bungled

their postcoital talk in the utility closet, Trey admitted that she had grounds to be upset. But not to hate him. Not to freeze him out with this ice-queen act of hers. He didn't deserve that.

Did he?

True, when she had confessed her virginity to him, he had been less than pleased with the revelation. He acknowledged that he should have managed a better response than shocked silence. His tense offer of marriage, if pregnancy dictated it, hadn't come out sounding very cordial, either.

Confiding his plan to marry at forty certainly hadn't helped any. He should have known better than to say a word about *that,* Trey glumly conceded. He'd learned years ago that his determination to stay single till age forty aggravated a wide range of people and was usually careful not to mention it anymore.

But with Callie he'd heedlessly blurted it out. The woman had a wildly unsettling effect on him. When he was with her he dropped his guard all too easily, and that was putting it mildly.

His behavior leading up to their flinch-worthy scene in the utility closet still appalled him. He remembered how he'd run after her, not thinking at all, simply acting out his feelings of wanting her, needing her. Taking the insanely stupid risk of not using protection. *Twice!*

Although Callie was not solely without blame herself, Trey reminded himself when the guilt and remorse became too hard to handle. He hadn't taken anything that she had not willingly given to him.

Furthermore, she was a nurse who knew as much about birth control as he did, for godsakes! No, their current estrangement wasn't *all* his fault.

So Trey spent three perfectly hideous days and nights vacillating between being furious with himself and furious with her, from accusing and absolving himself to accusing and absolving Callie.

He could hardly stand to look at her, it hurt so much, but he couldn't stop watching her because he was hotter for her than he had ever been for any woman in his life.

Truly, he was not behaving like a Weldon. But then he wasn't the same old Trey anymore. Callie Sheely had transformed him into someone unpredictable...but perhaps more exciting? Trey pondered that subversive thought for a moment, then dismissed it and headed for the OR.

Nine

Though Callie made it a point to visit Doug Radocay in his hospital room each day, her parents asked her to accompany them on the night they planned to visit him. She knew that hospitals unnerved them, a fear inherited from their immigrant parents, who viewed hospitals as places where you went to die.

Both Jack and Nancy Sheely were quite open about "hating to go near that place," though paradoxically, they were very proud of Callie's nursing career.

"Mom, it's a short-term stay for Doug. You really don't have to go to the hospital, you can visit him after he's discharged, when he comes over to see his grandmother," Callie proposed.

"In this neighborhood we always visit our sick," her mother replied, sounding scandalized that Callie would dare to suggest otherwise. "We'll meet you in the hospital lobby at seven sharp."

So Callie dressed in appropriate neighborhood-visitor

garb—a khaki jumper with a white cotton shirt under it, her hair pulled back neatly with two tortoiseshell barrettes—and met her parents in the lobby.

She hadn't been expecting Bonnie and Kirby, but they were there, too: Kirby in his ubiquitous Pittsburgh Steelers football jersey and jeans, Bonnie in a short, tight, black, silky dress and three-inch heels. And a long, flowing black cape with a scarlet lining.

"Callie, you look very nice, as usual." Their mother embraced Callie. "Just look at what your sister insisted on wearing." Nancy Sheely glowered at Bonnie, who glowered right back.

"I'm meeting friends and going out right after I visit Doug, Mother," Bonnie said crossly. "Stop staring at me, Callie," she added, turning her glare on her sister.

"It's the cape," Callie admitted. "Is it Vampire Night at the Big Bang tonight?"

Kirby was still laughing and Bonnie was still sulking when the Sheely family arrived in Doug Radocay's balloon-and flower- and people-filled room.

It seemed that half the neighborhood was visiting Doug tonight. The Sheelys were quickly enveloped in the festive atmosphere in the room.

"It's like a block party in here," Doug's father said several times, his face wreathed in smiles of relief every time he looked at his recuperating son.

Callie's role as heroine, in getting the revered Dr. Weldon to see Doug and perform his miracle surgery, was duly noted an embarrassing number of times.

Finally, she managed to slip quietly to the back of the room to stand near the door when Jimmy arrived, a Mylar balloon in hand.

"Thought you could use one of these, Doug," joked Jimmy, tying the string to the back of a chair where at least a dozen other balloons were tied.

He soon wandered over to join Callie. "Bet kid sister's getup went over big with your mom."

"Oh, yes. Meanwhile, I'm still sweet Saint Callie." She groaned. "No wonder Bonnie can't stand me. Or Kirby, either. I'm shoved down their throats as this perfect example but I'm a…a big fraud."

Her voice caught, and to her horror, tears filled her eyes. She quickly blinked them away, but not before Jimmy caught a glimpse.

He looked at her with concern. "Hey, Cal, are you okay?"

She shook her head, then nodded, a sign of confusion that didn't escape Jimmy's watchful gaze.

He leaned down, lowering his voice so only she could hear. "Does this have anything to do with the rumors going around about you and Weldon?"

"Oh, no! Are there rumors going around?" Callie winced. "But how? Why? Are you sure? Leo and Quiana haven't mentioned a thing to me."

"L and Q are very protective of you, Callie. Whenever anybody asks them about you and Weldon, they get nasty. So people stopped asking, but they haven't stopped talking. It seems you two have been, well, seen together."

"Of course we've been seen together. We work together in the OR every day."

"Sure. But the gossip is about where *else* you were seen together. In the Squirrel Den. In the tunnel, with you riding on his back. In the, um, women's surgical locker room and—" he paused, staring down at the floor with sudden interest "—er, leaving a utility closet looking like—"

"Never mind, Jimmy!"

"It's also been noted that you two now seem to be going out of your way not to be seen alone, not to speak much to each other, which is considered proof that you're trying to keep your romance a secret."

"That's the dumbest thing I've heard in a long time, Jimmy."

"Hey, don't get mad at me, I'm just repeating what I've been hearing." He shrugged. "You know how it is around here, Callie. The hospital is sort of like our old neighborhood, a rumor factory in overdrive. If anyone does anything, everybody has to comment."

"I'm not doing anything," Callie protested. Not now, anyway, she didn't bother to add.

She didn't have to; Jimmy put together the pieces on his own.

"Did Weldon dump you? Cal, I'm so sorry. If the guy doesn't see how wonderful you are, he's a real jerk!"

Callie smiled wryly. "Don't try telling anybody in this room that. They think Trey Weldon is right up there with God."

"Well, we know he isn't." Jimmy put his arm around her. "He's a jerk. Go on, say it. It'll make you feel better. Dr. Dimarino knows these things. Say it."

"Yes, Doctor." She couldn't help but smile at him. Dr. Dimarino was the same old Jimmy she'd known for so long. "Trey Weldon is a jerk."

Her words hit Trey just as he walked into Doug Radocay's room.

Trey Weldon is a jerk. They seemed to reverberate inside his head, penetrating every recess in his brain, including the pain center. Especially there.

Trey gazed at Callie, who looked heartstoppingly irresistible, her dark eyes shining, her tempting, luscious mouth smiling the sweetest smile.

At Jim Dimarino. Who had his arm draped possessively around her.

Trey had never experienced the phenomenon of "seeing red." He'd always thought it was a cliché, an expression vaguely connected to bullfighting, but now he knew it actually existed apart from that.

As jealousy and anger surged through him, he swore he could see a thin haze of red surrounding Callie and Jimmy, and he knew it was visible to his eyes only. Because he was the only one inflamed by the sight of the chummy pair.

"It's bad form to insult your boss to his face, Miss Sheely," Trey said tightly, forcing himself to smile.

He would not give anyone the satisfaction of knowing that the sight of her with another man, especially the beloved Jimmy, hurt like hell.

Callie and Jimmy whirled around at the sound of his voice, both flushing when they saw him. Unless his red haze of fury had infiltrated their skin tones?

Trey sucked in his cheeks and gave up his pretense of a smile.

"Uh-oh," Jimmy moaned.

Callie opened her mouth to speak, then closed it. What could she say? She'd called him a jerk, he'd overheard and was angry. Words were pretty much superfluous at this point. Unless she apologized?

Her eyes met his, and an almost tangible tension crackled between them.

Callie thought of their passionate interlude in the utility room, and the atrociously awkward conversation following it. And for the past four days he had treated her like a stranger or, worse, a stranger he'd taken an instant dislike to.

He *was* a jerk! And she wasn't going to apologize to him unless he apologized first for—

Apologize for what? her pragmatic alter ego demanded. For not acting like the man of her dreams in a scene that shouldn't have happened? For not being enthralled by her loss of virginity and their mutual lack of birth control?

At least he'd been honest with her about everything. He had been aghast at their mutual lapse and admitted it, he'd even told her about his plan to wait until he was forty to marry. No, she couldn't accuse the man of dishonesty about his intentions toward her.

Callie caught her lower lip between her teeth as she mulled that over.

Okay, he didn't have to apologize to her, but there would be no apology to him from her, either.

"Dr. Weldon!" called out one of the Radocays, spotting Trey. He was swept away into the crowd, eventually ending up at Doug's bedside.

"I wanted to see you tonight because you're being discharged in the morning, Doug," Trey explained. "Looks like you're already having a going-away party in here."

"And you're the guest of honor, Dr. Weldon," exclaimed old Mrs. Radocay. She linked her arm through Trey's with grandmotherly affection.

Callie was watching. She saw the odd expression momentarily flash across the older woman's face. Moments later her eyes connected with Callie's.

"Think ol' Mrs. R. picked up some vibes about you and Dr. Jerk?" Jimmy asked sympathetically, observing the scene.

Callie thought exactly that. When Trey left the room— without speaking to Callie again, without even glancing in her direction—she braced herself for Mrs. Radocay's inevitable interrogation.

It came after Callie had made her goodbyes to everyone and was preparing to leave the room. Mrs. Radocay followed her out into the hall and took her hand.

"Callie, why is your boyfriend so unhappy?"

Callie debated pretending that she didn't know who or what Mrs. R. was talking about, then discarded the idea. Mrs. Radocay was not one to be easily dissuaded, as she well knew.

"He's not my boyfriend, Mrs. Radocay." That was certainly true. When her reply was met with silence, Callie felt compelled to go on. "Romance in the workplace is like walking through a minefield. It's—you know—it's not a good thing to do."

"No, it isn't that at all," Mrs. Radocay insisted. "It's something else, Callie. You love him but—"

"I…care about him, but it's not mutual," Callie put in, blushing. "He…he doesn't want to get involved, especially not with me."

Mrs. Radocay gave a scornful snort. "You can't just sit back and expect things to happen, you have to be proactive."

"Proactive?" Callie echoed incredulously. It wasn't a word she would've expected a woman nearing ninety to toss off so easily.

Mrs. Radocay shrugged at Callie's surprised stare. "Now, you make things right with our wonderful Dr. Weldon. Be a nice girl and make it easy for him to be with you."

"Mrs. Radocay, I'm surprised at you," Callie mock-scolded her. "That's advice right from those retro dating manuals, when females were supposed to dedicate their every waking minute to landing a man, while the male target never had to do anything but breathe."

"All he needs is a little encouragement from you, Callie."

"Believe me, he's already had plenty. Those retro dating manuals would probably say he's already had too much. They recommend playing hard to get because men like the chase. Well, I don't want to shock you, Mrs. R., but I wasn't all that hard to get," she added darkly.

Mrs. Radocay appeared completely unshocked. "He's lonely, Callie. I could feel it. He needs you."

Callie's faith in Mrs. Radocay's perceptive ability was fading by the minute. She'd spent the past four days being snubbed by Trey Weldon, who was as self-assured and self-controlled as always.

What he wasn't—and what he would never be—was lonely and needy.

* * *

Trey hung around the nurses' station, glancing over patients' charts, though there had been no changes since he had updated each one a few hours ago. Well, he'd always prided himself on being thorough.

When Callie left Doug Radocay's room, he watched her, waiting for good old Jimmy to faithfully follow. But only the elderly grandmother emerged to have a few moments of intense conversation with Callie.

Trey released the breath he suddenly realized he'd been holding.

Callie walked to the bank of elevators and stepped into one of the cars. When she stepped out of it down in the lobby, Trey was already there. He watched her walk through the lobby and out the front entrance. And followed her.

He was not stalking her, Trey assured himself. He had gone to the lobby on a hunch. If she'd driven her car and parked in the adjacent garage, she would have gotten off the elevator at a different level.

But he strongly suspected she might have walked from her apartment, and he'd been right.

Walking around the city alone at night was simply not safe, especially not for a young woman. A beautiful, desirable young woman...who might be carrying his child.

Trey quickened his pace, keeping Callie in his sight while carefully keeping himself out of her awareness zone. He'd been raised a gentleman. He had an obligation to see her safely home.

He stood a slight distance away and watched as she unlocked the front door of her apartment building. She'd made it home safely, without requiring his assistance. Now she was about to enter the building and go upstairs to her apartment and he could leave...

"Callie, wait!" he heard himself call.

She turned, her dark eyes widening in surprise as he strode to stand just below the small porch. "I didn't know—"

"No, you didn't know I was following you, you didn't know *anybody* was following you," he cut in sternly. "You were completely unaware, blind to all danger. What if I'd been a…a mugger? When I saw you leave the lobby alone, I felt an obligation to follow you. I was raised a gentleman, you know," he added stiffly.

"I know. It's not something I'm likely to forget. Well, thank you for potentially rescuing me from a potential mugger. Or worse."

"I'm not about to go looking for another scrub nurse."

"And they claim that chivalry is dead." Callie smirked.

Trey was staring at her mouth. He couldn't tear his eyes away from it. Her beautifully shaped mouth. He remembered how it felt opening under his, he remembered how she tasted, sweet and hot and—

He swallowed hard, then cleared his throat. "We haven't had a chance to talk at the hospital for the past few days."

"No, we haven't." She was staring at him and quickly averted her eyes when he caught her looking at him.

"There is an important conversation that we haven't had." Trey stepped up on the small porch to stand beside her. It was really not much bigger than a doorstep, putting the two of them in close proximity indeed. "It's one we need to have, Callie. About the, uh, consequences of—"

"There are no consequences," she interjected quickly. "I told you there wouldn't be."

"Do you mean that you—"

"Do I have to spell it out for you?" She glared at him, her cheeks hot with color.

"Yes."

"I got my period the day before yesterday, just as predicted," she informed him briskly, clenching her fingers into fists. "We were lucky, so consider yourself off the hook, Trey."

"Lucky," he repeated flatly.

"Did you really expect it to be otherwise? You live a

charmed life, Trey. You always have. I have no doubt that you'll meet the love of your life at age thirty-nine, marry her at forty and have brilliant, beautiful children whenever you choose to. You live a charmed life,'' she repeated wistfully.

"I haven't lived a charmed life," he was quick to counter. "You don't know—"

"Oh, yes, you did have to suffer through the misery of Miss Martha's dancing lessons all those years ago." Her lips twisted into a wry smile. "Since you hate dancing so much, that probably means you're not very good at it. And being less than perfect at anything would be unacceptable to you. Okay, I guess that means you've lived a *semi* charmed life."

Their eyes met and held for a long moment.

Then Callie looked away, turning her attention to the door. Her key was still in the lock and she removed it, pushing open the door. "Good night, Trey. You can go home happy, your freedom is safe. I'll see you in the morning."

Trey frowned. She was withdrawing from him, both physically and emotionally. For a few brief moments they'd been connected again despite her flare of temper. Now she was shutting him out again.

He felt a civil war brewing within himself. She was right. He should go home and stop worrying that he would be married before his time, the result of a regretted, impulsive act. Except what he was regretting now was not having the opportunity to, well, act impulsively once more.

"You could invite me in for coffee," he said before he could stop himself.

"How can I put this tactfully?" Callie gave him a look that would have leveled a lesser man. "Hmm, I can't, so I'll just say it outright. No way in hell, Trey."

"Are you afraid to be alone with me?" Trey knew he was taunting her; he just wasn't sure why.

Well perhaps he did have an inkling.

"I would think *you* would be afraid to be alone with *me*."

She matched his baiting tone, her dark eyes mocking. "After all, you just narrowly escaped a fate worse than death, didn't you? Imagine having to marry seven years earlier than your carefully calculated schedule allows—and with a pregnant prole as your bride! How absolutely horrifying that would've been for you! And how very unWeldon."

"You certainly can take it—and dish it out," he mused aloud.

A warm glow of admiration, mingled with affection, suddenly surged through him. It was a heady feeling, and standing so close to her increased it exponentially. The days of coldness between them had taken their toll on him. Now even the heat of her anger warmed him, made him feel—

"Oh, dear!" Callie exclaimed suddenly.

She had glanced around him and was now looking up the street.

Trey quickly whirled around, following her gaze. On the sidewalk he saw a man in his midforties, average height, average build and wearing an inexpensive suit, hurrying toward them carrying a brown grocery bag.

"Mom forgot to give you the bread she baked for you, honey-bunch," the man called, holding out the bag. "I told her I'd run it down to you."

"It's my dad," murmured Callie. "Goodbye, Trey."

Trey stayed put. "I've never met your father. I'd like to," he added, ignoring her forbidding eyes. *She didn't want him to meet her father!* The revelation came as something of a shock to him. He couldn't remember the last time anyone had been reluctant to introduce him to somebody.

Callie didn't wait for her father to join them, she hurried to meet him. Trey approached the two as Mr. Sheely was handing over the grocery bag to his daughter.

"Hello, I'm Trey Weldon." He introduced himself to the older man and extended his hand to shake.

"Jack Sheely." Jack shook Trey's hand vigorously.

"Sure, I recognize you from young Doug's room a little while ago, Dr. Weldon. You're a hero around our neighborhood for saving Doug."

"Your daughter deserves credit for encouraging me to take the case," Trey replied smoothly. He knew he'd hit exactly the right note because Jack Sheely's smile lit up his face.

"Well, that's our Callie. She's always known what to do, and then she does it. No goofing off or messing up, no sir. Not her. Do you know we've never had one second of trouble with that girl since the day she was born?" Jack eyed his oldest child fondly.

"Thank Mom for the bread," Callie spoke up quickly. "And thanks for bringing it down, Dad. I'll talk to you both later in the week."

It was a clear dismissal, and Trey saw Mr. Sheely ready to obey his perfect daughter, to turn and leave.

"Callie and I were just going upstairs to her place to have coffee, Mr. Sheely. Perhaps you'll join us?" Trey nearly laughed out loud at Callie's expression, a combination of stunned indignation and...panic?

"Dad, you have to get back to the hospital. Mom's waiting there for you, isn't she?"

"As a matter of fact, Kirby drove Mommy home. Bonnie's still up there but I don't expect she'll care if I have a quick cup with you two. Callie makes great coffee," he added, beaming up at Trey. "She's a good cook, too. Learned from her mom who's one of the best."

Oh, Lord, it was already starting. Callie tried not to hyperventilate.

She'd known that introducing Trey Weldon to her parents would be disastrous from the moment the older Sheelys had inadvertently learned—from Jimmy, the rat!—that her boss was single, not even engaged, which to them equaled totally eligible.

Jack and Nancy Sheely saw no class barriers, and Callie

didn't want to risk hurting their feelings by pointing out that the Weldons and the Sheelys were like separate species who could not mix. She had been vigilant about not mentioning Trey, except in reference to her job, and giving vague answers to their too-direct questions about him.

Knowing her parents' increasing preoccupation with weddings and grandchildren, she had been fully aware of the consequences should they ever meet "the bachelor doctor."

Still, she had never expected it to happen. Why would it? Trey and the Sheelys all but lived in separate universes; their orbits were most unlikely to intersect.

Except it had happened, and Trey himself had instigated it. Callie caught his eye. He grinned at her, looking smug, like he'd just outsmarted her. Well, he would be sorry!

She flashed him a malicious little smile. True, she was about to be heartily embarrassed, but Trey would find the encounter both awkward and boring. *Which only served him right!*

"Do you know my niece Mary Jo—she's my brother Bob's oldest girl—is married to a neurosurgeon?" Jack Sheely asked Trey as the three of them trooped upstairs to Callie's apartment. "Did Callie ever mention that to you?"

"Really?" replied Trey, sounding interested. "No, Callie never mentioned it."

Callie could tell, by his most subtle inflections, when his *really* conveyed feigned or genuine interest. She knew he was faking it right now.

But Jack Sheely needed no encouragement, either real or faux.

"Yeah, Mary Jo is a nurse, too, just like Callie, but she doesn't work anymore since she and her husband Steve have a baby girl, Elissa. My brother is a grandfather, that lucky duck. That makes me a great-uncle, which is nice but not the same as having your own grandkids, you know?"

"You look much too young to be a great-uncle," Trey said tactfully.

Callie turned her attention to the coffee making, but her apartment was too small for her not to hear every word her father said.

"And isn't it a coincidence that both the Sheely girls who are nurses, Mary Jo and my Callie, worked with neurosurgeons?" Jack continued.

"An interesting coincidence," Trey mumbled.

"Actually, that's how Mary Jo met her husband," continued Jack. "She worked in the neuro intensive care unit, taking care of his patients. She and Steve worked so well together, it was just natural that they would get along outside the hospital, too. Their wedding and the reception was really something!"

Callie couldn't bring herself to meet Trey's eyes. She served the coffee in mugs, milk and sugar in her father's, black for her and Trey.

"Trey isn't interested in weddings or in getting married, Dad," Callie said. It was past time to derail this runaway train of a topic. "It's not for him or his life-style. If you know what I mean," she added pointedly, gazing directly into her father's eyes.

Jack Sheely looked startled. And then comprehension began to dawn, visibly, on his face. "Ohhh! Sure, yes, I know." He nodded his head vigorously. "And, uh, I don't want you to think I'm some kind of prejudiced type, Doc. I'm not! Your, um, private life is your own business. And I can tell you don't deliberately flaunt your, er, life-style. I can respect that."

He cast a quick, uncertain glance at his daughter, who gave him an approving, encouraging smile. Callie almost laughed out loud as she saw Trey fully comprehend her father's declaration.

He opened his mouth to speak, but Jack Sheely preempted him.

"I better go get Bonnie up at the hospital," Jack explained, rising to his feet. "She has plans for tonight. You know the young people and their plans.'' He left his coffee untouched in the mug.

Callie walked him to the door. ''Good night, Dad. And thanks for stopping by.''

''Glad to. 'Night, honey-bunch.'' He gave Callie a quick kiss on her cheek and then nodded in Trey's direction. ''It was very nice meeting you, Dr. Weldon.'' But his avid interest in the ''bachelor doctor'' was clearly at an end.

Callie closed the door behind him, turning to find Trey glaring accusingly at her.

''You led your father to believe I was gay!'' he exclaimed indignantly.

She shrugged. ''Did I? I was referring to your plans to stay single till you're forty, but I guess Dad could've misinterpreted me.''

''You knew he would! You meant him to. I saw that... that glance you gave him. Your eyes are so expressive they can practically talk!''

''Maybe they speak a different language than my tongue does,'' Callie suggested with a shrug. ''Anyway, it doesn't matter, does it?''

''Hell, yes, it matters!'' Trey stormed toward her and kept coming until her back was up against the door.

''Why? You won't ever see my father again. Why should you care what he thinks about you?''

Trey paused a moment, as if to consider it. ''I don't want him spreading lies about me to the Radocays, my patient's family. And you ought to know by now that I don't like gossip of any kind, so I certainly wouldn't want to be the hospital grapevine's latest hot topic. I'm sure your pal Jimmy would be eager to gleefully pass along what your father now thinks is—''

''Jimmy knows you're not gay,'' Callie said. ''I'll explain all about tonight to him, if you'd like. He knows how relentless my parents can be. *His* are the same way when it comes to getting him married off. He'll understand completely.''

"Jimmy is just the soul of understanding, isn't he?'' growled Trey.

Callie felt light-headed. Their position, toe-to-toe, with Trey mere inches in front of her, sandwiching her between him and the door, was all too reminiscent of those two memorable times they'd both lost it and ended up making love.

"I know how much you hate gossip, but unfortunately you're already a hot topic at the hospital.'' Callie focused her gaze on the lamp across the room. She didn't dare risk looking into Trey's blue eyes and losing herself there as she'd done before.

Better to distract him with information sure to disturb him. "We both are. Jimmy says there is a lot of talk about you and me and—''

"Well then, as the song goes, 'Let's give them something to talk about.'''

Instead of being outraged about the gossip, Trey abruptly clasped her head with both his hands and covered her mouth with his, increasing the pressure until her lips parted and she granted him entry.

He drove his tongue into her mouth, kissing her fully and deeply, as if he were starving for her.

Callie surrendered with a shuddering sigh, leaning in against him, putting her arms around him to cuddle closer.

She heard him groan, felt his hands gliding over her back, then around to cup one breast in his palm. She couldn't keep herself from pressing her breast firmly into the big warm palm of his hand.

Though she feared that his touch could easily become an addictive pleasure, the contact felt so good that right now she didn't care.

His other hand tugged at the zipper of her jumper, and he lifted his lips, holding them an inch or two above her own.

"I am not gay," he enunciated each word. "I want you so much that I—"

"No." Callie pulled away from him, gulping for air. Her jumper was already completely unzipped, and she quickly set to straightening her clothing with trembling fingers.

The brief break in kissing had allowed her to stop and think, and though it wasn't easy, she tried to jump-start her muddled brain into working correctly again. "Doesn't something about this whole scene strike you as familiar?" Her voice was shaky and breathless. "Way too familiar."

"Callie—" He took a step toward her. And another.

"Just stay where you are," she ordered. "Better yet, leave. Right now."

She began to gather the three untouched mugs of coffee and carry them into her tiny kitchen area.

"If you don't go home now, I can predict exactly what will happen, and I don't have a shred of Mrs. Radocay's psychic ability. I don't need it. We're caught in the same cycle and I don't—"

"Don't bother telling me you don't want me. I know you do, Callie. You were with me all the way."

She regarded him thoughtfully. "One thing I've learned is that a person doesn't always get what they want, Trey. I can see that someone like you might not have had to face that lesson yet, but—"

"Someone like me?" His voice deepened ominously. "What does that mean?"

"That you have everything and always have had, and that you haven't run across the word, *can't* very often. If ever. But I'm saying it now, Trey, and I want you to hear me. We can't have sex again tonight."

As much as she wanted him, as much as she loved him, she was not going to indulge in another rash act and then have to endure more torturous days of loss and pain and regret like the past four.

"Can't? You mean you *won't*," he amended, studying her.

"That's right."

His blue eyes held a rakish gleam. "Because it's a certain time of the month and you're far too inhibited to let me—"

"Get out!"

"Callie, I was kidding. I—"

"If you don't leave right now, I'll…I'll—" She tried to think what she would do if he wouldn't leave.

"Are you thinking about throwing that coffee at me?" Trey was watching as her fingers absently curled around the handle of one of the mugs.

Callie looked down to see herself gripping the mug, though tossing it hadn't occurred to her. "I was the pitcher on the girls' softball team all through school, and I have really good aim, so if I threw it at you, I wouldn't miss."

"A good athlete, smart, beautiful. No wonder you're the apple of your parents' eye. *You're* the one who's lived a charmed life, Callie."

Callie wondered if he was being snide, but his voice, his expression, held no trace of it.

"Not hardly!" She laughed a little. "Sometimes my dad gets carried away and forgets that I was not the perfect angel he thinks he remembers. I certainly haven't been angelic around you lately," she added pointedly.

"That's my fault." Trey swallowed hard. "You have nothing more to worry about, Callie. I'm back in control of myself and I apologize for—"

"It was my fault, too," she said quickly, unwilling to let him shoulder all the blame. "But now we're back to being our normal selves."

"Which is a good thing, but certainly not thrilling or passionate."

His tone sounded—questioning?—to her.

Callie decided she must've imagined it. After all, he'd told her himself about his plans for his future, and they did not include her.

"Thrills and passion do not belong in a professional relationship," she said, knowing it was what he wanted to hear, what was best for her to keep in mind. "And that's the only kind we can have."

Ten

Thrills and passion do not belong in a professional relationship, and that's the only kind we can have.

Back in his own apartment a short while later, Callie's edict kept echoing in Trey's head the way a bad song does, over and over, as if permanently stuck there. Every time he tried to distract himself by thinking of something else, *Thrills and passion do not belong in a professional relationship and that's the only kind we can have* would intrude once again.

It was exceedingly annoying.

Restlessly he wandered through his sparsely furnished four rooms noticing, as if for the first time, the complete lack of any personalizing touches.

He found himself comparing his place to Callie's.

His apartment was bigger, but she'd made a real home of hers, complete with photos and cheerful colors and all sorts of things that individualized it as her own. He had a bed and a chest of drawers for his clothes, a nondescript sofa and a TV set in the living room, though he rarely turned it on.

Basically his was a place to sleep and nothing else. Homey touches in whatever rooms he happened to be occupying just weren't of interest to him. His career had always been the focal point of his existence, to the exclusion of all else.

When he married at forty, he would buy a house, and his new wife could decorate it in tasteful Weldon manner. Until then he didn't care how barren his living quarters were.

Thrills and passion do not belong in a professional relationship, and that's the only kind we can have.

Tonight his apartment looked depressingly bleak to him. Trey scowled, exasperated with himself, feeling the unwelcome stirrings of self-pity. A most unattractive state.

He attempted to reason it all away. His apartment looked exactly the way it had the entire time he'd lived there, not one thing had changed. It looked like every other functional but dull place he'd lived since leaving the large, gracious Weldon home in Virginia.

The phone rang and he rushed to answer it, grateful for the diversion. Despite his aversion to self-pity, he was beginning to feel the way his apartment looked. Bleak and lonely.

Trey snatched up the receiver without bothering to glance at the caller ID box. "Mother?" The sound of his mother's voice on the other end of the line surprised him.

"Your father and I are coming to visit you. We feel quite remiss that we haven't been to Pittsburgh and seen your new home and hospital yet. We want to remedy that very soon. Would you mind?"

"Of course not. I've love to have you and Dad visit."

Trey glanced at the bare white walls. His mother would lament the Spartan decor, as she did in every place he had lived since he'd left home. It depressed her, she would say.

Perhaps he would buy a few pictures and hang them so the room wouldn't look so...stark.

"And in a marvelous coincidence, some old friends of ours will be visiting relatives in Pittsburgh that very same weekend." Trey tuned back in to hear his mother say, "The Walshes, John and Betsy. You remember them."

Trey wasn't sure. He had never spent much time with his parents' friends; his customary excuse was that he was too busy studying to socialize. It had always served as an excellent out because his parents and their friends were endlessly trying to set him up with "the right girl."

They still were. Older now and long out of school, he used his burgeoning career and consequent tight schedule as an excuse to avoid the matchmaking attempts.

Trey thought of Jack Sheely, so blatantly bragging about Callie's virtues and abilities. It was mortifying, but probable, that his mother similarly tried to "sell" him to women she considered suitable candidates for him.

Trey almost smiled when he thought of how Callie had discouraged her father. It seemed funny and inventive now, creative and quick thinking on her part. He wished he'd laughed with her about it after Jack Sheely's departure.

Thrills and passion do not belong in a professional relationship and that's the only kind we can have. Trey ground his teeth in vexation. Sharing a laugh was permitted in a professional relationship.

He really should have laughed with Callie. Instead, he'd gotten angry like a sour, humorless boor. Jimmy Dimarino would have laughed.

"Springtime Ball," he heard his mother say.

Trey's mind had totally drifted from their conversation. But anything ending in *ball* was sure to mean trouble. *"What?"*

"Oh, Trey, please don't fuss at me. I know you claim not to like dancing but Betsy's sister-in-law, Anne, said the Springtime Ball sponsored by their hospital auxiliary is great fun. It's a wonderful fund-raiser with lovely mix of guests. Naturally, your father and I want to go along with the Walshes and their relatives since we'll be in town, and of course we want our handsome son there with us,'' Laura Weldon added with her usual enthusiasm.

''Mother, I am—''

''Betsy says that Anne knows several wonderful young women whom she would love to introduce to you, Trey. You can take one of them to the ball and sit at our table.''

''A blind date? I hope you're joking, Mother. I believe I've given you my opinion on blind dates countless times, and it hasn't changed.''

''It wouldn't exactly be a blind date, Trey. You could meet each girl first, look her over and then take the one of your choice.''

''You make it sound like choosing a puppy from a litter!''

His mother didn't try to disguise her exasperated sigh. ''Trey, I hate to be blunt but—well, I suppose I'm going to have to be. You're certainly blunt with me. Son, you are thirty-three years old. I'm fifty-four. I want grandchildren, and not when I'm too old to enjoy them.''

''You *have* a grandchild. Win and Parker Lee—''

''Little Chip is adorable and I love him, but I want my own son to have a child of his own.''

''Be careful what you wish for, Mother,'' Trey warned.

She didn't know how close she'd come to becoming a grandma, and he was tempted to tell her. He didn't give in to the urge, but the very fact that he'd had such a renegade impulse unnerved him.

''Does that mean what I think it might?'' Laura Weldon sounded downright hopeful.

It occurred to Trey that his mother wouldn't be shocked or disapproving if he'd made Callie pregnant, thus obligating him to marry her. She probably would be delighted! It was so very unWeldon, but then, his mother had not been born a Weldon, she'd married into the family.

And brought him into it with her. Trey took a deep, painful breath.

"I don't need you or your friends to get me a date, Mother," he said in a stern, forbidding tone that had rattled a fair share of underlings subjected to it.

His mother remained unaffected. "This is getting better and better. It sounds to me as though you have a girlfriend up there, Trey. Trust you to keep it a deep dark secret! I can't wait to meet her. I'll just go ahead and tell Betsy Walsh you'll be attending the ball with your date."

"What can anybody tell me about this Springtime Ball?" Trey asked the group assembled the next morning in the OR, before beginning to resect an aneurysm on his already anesthetized patient.

He directed the question to no one in particular, but his eyes met Callie's as she handed him the scalpel he wanted. Before he had to ask for it, of course.

He expected her to reply, but it was Quiana Turner who supplied the answer.

"It's the hospital party of the year. Just about everybody on the staff goes. You were here at Tri-State last year, Doc. Didn't you go to the ball?" quizzed Quiana.

"No, I didn't."

"Gee, I wonder why not?" Callie sounded ingenuously innocent as she handed Trey a tiny gauze sponge before he knew he was going to need it. "There is always a great band and dancing."

"There's a terrific buffet and open bar, too," Leo added, apparently trying to help Callie sell the idea of attending the ball to Trey.

Only Callie and Trey knew she was mocking his dislike of such affairs.

A shared private joke. Allowable in a professional relationship, although thrills and passion weren't.

"My wife is a member of the hospital auxiliary who sponsors it. The ball brings in a lot of money that goes to the hospital for special projects,'' said the anesthesiologist.

"Interesting. Maybe I'll go this year." Trey noted with satisfaction Callie's startled dark eyes.

He dropped the conversation and focused his attention on the delicate surgery. It was a long arduous operation, with Trey explaining the procedure step by step and questioning the students throughout.

Finally the surgery was successfully completed, and Trey moved back from the table, motioning for the neurosurgical resident to close.

"Since this Springtime Ball is a major fund-raiser for the hospital, I suppose I ought to go." Trey picked up the conversation he had earlier abandoned for his surgical instruction, right where he'd left off.

Instead of leaving the OR as he usually did upon completing the surgery, he stood beside Callie and watched the resident do the routine closing. He noticed her attention was riveted on the patient and felt a warm streak of pride as she subtly offered the young doctor in training guidance based on her own considerable OR experience.

"You really should go, Doc," Leo agreed. "The whole OR gang will be there. You can hang with us. Isn't that incentive enough?"

"If it's not, keep in mind all the food you can eat plus that free, open bar. There's something called a Chinese auction, too," Quiana added encouragingly.

"You've all convinced me to go," Trey announced. "As long as dancing with two left feet is tolerated."

"Oh, Dr. Weldon, I think you're just being modest," said an admiring medical student, as the patient was whisked away to the recovery room.

Callie covertly glanced at the young woman. Though she couldn't be sure because of the surgical cap and mask, the student's glowing eyes and gushing tone seemed very familiar. Chances were good she was that same girl who'd fawned all over Trey the other day.

Once again Callie tried not to notice. Trey would always have his hero-worshipers, and the younger they were the more she discounted them. She knew Trey well enough to know that he would consider any student off-limits. He was no womanizing predator and never would be.

She joined the others leaving the OR, moving quickly to slip around Trey and his admirer, unobserved.

"You are so amazingly well coordinated, I can't believe you aren't a wonderful dancer, too, Dr. Weldon," the student all but purred.

"Well, believe it," Callie heard Trey say. "I'm not."

She was already in front of the pair, on her way to catch up to Quiana and Leo.

"It's charming that you have a fault and own up to it, Dr. Weldon," the medical student cooed at the same moment Callie came to an abrupt dead stop.

She hadn't planned to. But someone had grasped her upper arm, halting her in her tracks. Callie jerked her head around to see Trey's outstretched arm, his hand gripping her.

A split second later he was directly behind her.

"Are you brave enough to risk dancing with me, Callie?" he asked rather jauntily.

The medical student immediately moved on, without another word. Callie saw everybody else sneaking glances at her and Trey.

She turned around and faced him, but that move brought her so close to him that her breasts brushed his chest. Callie flushed and quickly jumped back. Trey remained where he was, watching her flustered reaction.

It was not fair that he could remain so implacable while she was as jittery as a Victorian maiden around him! Callie was determined to regain her composure—or to make him lose some of his.

"If you're trying to discourage your adoring fan, I don't

appreciate being used as the decoy,'' she muttered testily, pulling off her gloves.

Trey had already discarded his mask and gloves, and he reached up to remove her mask. ''I can hardly hear you with that thing on.''

The touch of his fingers made her quiver. And had she imagined it, or did his fingertips linger on her nape longer than the task required?

Callie looked up at him. He did not appear to be at all affected by their close proximity, which only heightened her irritation. ''You can hear me very well with it on. You've never had trouble hearing anything I say in the OR.''

He made no comment and proceeded to pull off her cap and discard it.

Her fingers automatically combed through her hair in an attempt to unflatten her dark tresses. Then she realized that Trey might think she was primping for *him*—which was not the case at all!—and she let her hands fall to her sides.

''Well, will you go?''

''You're asking me to the Springtime Ball?'' Callie was incredulous.

''I've never known you to be this slow, Sheely. Your blood sugar must be low, you need something to eat right now. Yes, I am asking you to the Springtime Ball.''

She folded her arms in front of her and gazed up at him. ''Is this a joke?''

''Do I look as if I'm joking?''

Callie silently conceded that he did not appear to be even slightly jovial. ''You hate gossip, Trey,'' she felt obliged to remind him. ''You have to realize that you're adding fuel to the fire by…this. If we went to the ball, it would—''

''*When* we go to the ball,'' he corrected. ''Say yes, Callie.''

She eyed him skeptically. ''What brought on this sudden change of heart? About—the ball, I mean,'' she added, her cheeks flushing.

"I'm glad you clarified that, Sheely. Otherwise I might've thought you were referring to our decision to keep our relationship professional."

Callie didn't miss the sarcasm in his tone. "Tell me what is really going on, Trey. We've always been open and honest with each other."

Well, she'd been partially open and honest with him, she admitted to herself, because being secretly in love with a man didn't meet the criterion for fully open or fully honest.

"You want full disclosure?" Trey heaved a sigh. "Okay, here it is. My parents will be in town visiting friends who are patrons of the Springtime Ball. I am expected to appear—with a date in tow. If I don't supply my own, one will be provided for me. I can't tell you how much I detest blind dates."

"Even more than you hate dancing?" Callie laughed; she couldn't help it. "So even the mighty Trey Weldon is susceptible to parental pressure? Who knew?"

"I'm glad you find this so amusing. We'll be at a table with my parents and their friends, but of course, we won't have to stay there all evening. We can, uh, hang with the OR crowd if you'd like."

Callie tried to imagine sitting at a table eating dinner with the Weldons and their socially prominent Pittsburgh friends. What on earth would they talk about? She had nothing at all in common with that crowd.

An even worse scenario presented itself—an uncomfortable, even hostile silence, with the wealthy Weldons and their friends snubbing her as an opportunistic social-climbing tramp from the wrong side of the tracks.

Why put herself through a hellish evening like that? The answer was obvious: she wouldn't.

"Trey, this isn't a good idea. But, um, thank you for the invitation," she added, remembering her manners. She could be as polite as any socialite!

Callie walked off, leaving a thunderstruck Trey behind.

Not for long.

"You're turning down my invitation?" He stopped her in front of the door to the women's locker room, staring down at her with disbelief.

"I've never known you to be this slow, Dr. Weldon. Your blood sugar must be low, you need something to eat right now. Yes, I am turning down your invitation to the Springtime Ball."

She smiled sweetly, as if she hadn't just flung his own flippant response right back at him.

She'd said no.

Now it was *that* stunning realization that played repetitiously in Trey's head, supplanting the odious *Thrills and passion do not belong in a professional relationship and that's the only kind we can have,* that had been stuck there.

It could be argued that one was the logical offshoot of the other. But Trey preferred to look at the situation from a different angle.

Why couldn't two congenial colleagues in a professional relationship attend a ball together? How did that differ from two professionals having lunch or dinner or a friendly game of golf together?

Callie's refusal made less and less sense the more Trey thought about it. Which was almost constantly from the time he arrived back at his apartment that evening.

He prolonged leaving the hospital, catching up on paperwork, reviewing patients' charts, making another round of private visits to his patients and chatting more personally with them, easier to do without the crowd of learners who accompanied him on daily grand rounds.

Finally, he trekked through the tunnel to visit the Hagen boy, whose condition remained unchanged from the surgery following his accident. Critical but stable. The boy's mother remained at his bedside, and Trey tried to offer her a few words of hope.

But now here he was, back in his bleak, boring apartment with nothing to do. There was nothing on television he felt like watching, there were no books he felt like reading, he was all caught up on his medical journals.

She'd said no.

He thought about that stupid ball, with himself escorting a young woman selected by his parents' friends. She might be a very nice person—undoubtedly she would be—but she would not be Callie Sheely.

Callie would be "hanging with the OR crowd," laughing and dancing and having fun. Trey didn't even have to close his eyes to picture her dancing with Jimmy Dimarino, slow dancing to a romantic ballad.

He saw it clearly in his mind's eye, and that was bad enough. To have to actually watch it happen...

Half an hour later Trey pulled his black Porsche Carrera in front of the old renovated Victorian house that had been converted into apartments. He saw the lights on in Callie's second-floor living room.

Finding a parking place directly in front of the building seemed like a good omen, if he believed in such things—which he did not. Suddenly, coming over here seemed as pointless and foolish as it had when he'd first decided to do it while pacing aimlessly through his stark, sterile apartment.

"Cool car." Jimmy Dimarino, wearing hospital whites, was walking toward him, his gaze affixed to Trey's car.

Trey didn't bother to ask if he'd been with Callie, just as Jimmy didn't ask if Trey had come to see her. The answers were all too obvious.

"I'll never have a car like that," Jimmy said wistfully, his eyes not leaving the sports car. "I have so many med school loans to pay off that I'll be driving the old Chevy my granddad gave me until it falls apart. Then I'll have to get around by bus."

Trey did not point out that his own education had been

paid by his trust fund, and he had accrued no debts at all. Boasting about financial security was not the Weldon way.

"Good luck cooling off Callie," Jimmy said, running a hand through his wiry black hair. He smiled grimly. "Although I, uh, don't think you came over to do that, did you?"

Trey's eyes narrowed. "What are you trying to say, Dimarino?"

"Callie is mad." Jimmy looked inordinately glum. "I mean, really *really* furious. I haven't seen her this mad since we were in junior high and a bunch of us guys in the neighborhood teased Mrs. Plasky's cat and it ran up the tree and got stuck there. Callie told Mrs. Plasky, who called the cops and the fire department, and then she went to every one of our houses and told our mothers. Callie did, not Mrs. Plasky," he added.

Trey stared at him, nonplussed. "Did the cat get down safely?" he wondered aloud.

"Yeah, Callie's dad—he's a fireman, you know—got him down. Then he read each one of us the riot act." Jimmy shook his head. "You and Callie are a lot alike, y' know. Worrying about that stupid cat. I guess she thinks I've done a lot worse this time," he added dejectedly.

Trey clenched his fists. "What did you do?"

Jimmy lowered his eyes and stared at the ground. "Last night I— Well, I was on call but I…spent some time with her sister. With Bonnie." He gulped. "Okay, I know I've known Bonnie since she was born, but she's not a kid anymore, believe me. Last night we got to talking in Doug Radocay's room, and then her dad left the hospital without her so she didn't have a ride, and all of a sudden one thing led to another—"

"And Callie is jealous?" Trey asked tersely.

"Jealous? Are you kidding? No, she's in full big-sister mode, accusing me of practically committing incest because I watched Bonnie grow up. Yeah, I watched her, all right.

It's Callie who's like my sister, with *her* it would be incest."
Jimmy gave a rueful laugh. "Bonnie is…different."

"Different? How?"

"She's bratty, she's slutty, she's wild," Jimmy burst out.
"She got kicked out of Guardian Angels High and had to
go to public high school. When I go back to the old neighborhood to visit my folks, she drops by, always teasing
and…and getting under my skin."

"I see." Trey nodded his head, feeling suddenly, incred-
ibly cheerful. He gave the younger man a fraternal pat on
the shoulder. "Callie ought to understand that sometimes
things happen that we don't plan."

"Do you think maybe you could talk to her about it?"
Jimmy looked hopeful. "I hate that our friendship is, well,
according to her, finished. Tell her she can't mean it. She'll
listen to you." He paused, frowning. "Hey, I just remembered—you dumped Callie, didn't you? Well, scratch that
idea, she probably won't let you in the door. Can things get
any worse?"

Trey decided not to say that, for himself, things had taken
an extraordinary turn for the better. It wasn't Weldon style
to rub his own good fortune in the face of the downtrodden.

Jimmy forlornly trudged off to his '85 Chevy parked up
the street. Trey pressed the outside buzzer to summon Callie
to let him in.

"Go away, Jimmy," she called over the intercom. "I told
you that I—"

"It's Trey. Let me in, Callie. It's starting to rain." Which
was true, although the overhang protected him from getting
wet.

The buzz sounded, and the lock on the front door was
released. Trey strode inside, bounding up the stairs two at a
time.

Callie had opened the door to her apartment and was
standing in front of it as he arrived on the second floor. His
eyes swept over her face. Jimmy was right; she was furious.

Her dark eyes were smoldering, and not with passion. With sheer rage. He had no trouble discerning the difference.

Trey decided that this might not be the ideal time to mention the Springtime Ball—if that's what he had come here to do. He was no longer sure of his precise motives for being here. He only knew he couldn't stay away from her any longer.

Why did he and Callie have to stay apart, anyway? Neither of them was involved with anyone else, neither of them wanted anyone else.

Why had they decided they couldn't have the thrills and passion of a personal relationship? He tried to remember, but the reasons eluded him. He no longer cared what they were.

"I guess I'll take that coffee I never seem to get around to drinking when I'm over here," he said lightly.

"It's too late for coffee, I'll make tea." Callie turned and went inside.

Trey followed her, closing the door behind her.

"If you're here to try to talk me into going to the Springtime Ball with you, forget it." Callie filled the teakettle with water and set it on a burner with a firm bang.

No, this wasn't a good time to discuss the Springtime Ball, but since she'd brought it up, he was stuck with it. Trey cleared his throat. "I have to admit the way I worded my invitation would not have won Miss Martha's stamp of approval. It sounded as though I'd asked you only to avoid having a blind date foisted on me and that I wouldn't have invited you otherwise."

"Which is true. And no, I won't go with you, not even to spare you the horrors of a blind date. It's…it's inappropriate for us to go together."

"Inappropriate," Trey repeated thoughtfully. "I saw Jimmy on the sidewalk and he mentioned that you think his, er, friendship with your sister is inappropriate."

"That weasel took my little sister down to the On Call quarters and...and laid her!" Callie exclaimed, her dark eyes flashing. "That is *not* friendship. Jimmy has known Bonnie since she was a baby, he used to pull her in his wagon when she was too tired to walk home from the cemetery with us. He—"

"Cemetery?" Trey interjected, startled. "Why were you there?"

"It's in the neighborhood. It was our playground," she explained quickly, eager to continue her litany. "When Bonnie got kicked out of Guardian Angels High, Jimmy was in college, and he came over to talk to her, to try to tell her how important it was for her future to do well in school. God knows she wouldn't listen to Mom or Dad or me. She didn't listen to Jimmy, either." Callie scowled. "Bonnie does exactly as she pleases."

"Callie, I don't know your sister, but I assume she is over twenty-one?" At her nod, he continued, "Then she is not a child, she's a consenting adult, especially if she does exactly as she pleases. And from what Jimmy said—" Trey walked over to her and cupped her cheek with his hand, feeling the silky softness of her skin "—it sounds as if an irresistible impulse overtook them last night. Much like the one that propelled you and me into that utility closet, perhaps?"

Callie stiffened and jerked her head away from his hand. "I don't want to talk about that. And why are you trying to defend Jimmy's actions? I didn't think you even liked him."

"I didn't when I thought he was in love with you," Trey said bluntly. "I was jealous as hell. But now that I know he's lusting after little sister, Bonnie, I feel downright charitable toward him. He's your good friend and he is distressed at the thought of losing your friendship, Callie."

"Well, that's just too bad!"

The teakettle began to whistle, and she prepared the tea. Trey watched her.

"How do you know I like one teaspoon of sugar in my

tea?'' he asked curiously when she handed him a cup. ''I don't think I've ever drunk tea with you.''

''Yes, you have. In the lounge when there was no coffee left. Of course, I'm sure that having tea there is nothing like having tea with your family. You probably have an heirloom teapot and those fancy little sandwiches and a servant who—''

''Do you have us confused with the British royal family? I'm from Virginia, not Buckingham Palace, Callie.''

He followed her to the sofa and sat down beside her, teacup in hand.

''I know you're not all that crazy about tea, but I guess you figured not accepting it from me tonight wasn't an option?'' Callie turned to him, her lips curved into a sudden wry smile.

''Pretty much.'' Trey set the teacup on the coffee table. ''Callie, would you consider listening to the new, improved version of my invitation to that damnable ball?''

She rolled her eyes. ''You're off to a great start. Who wouldn't want to go to a damnable ball?''

Smiling, Trey took her teacup from her and set it on the table next to his. He took her hand in his. ''Would you do me the honor of allowing me to be your escort to the Springtime Ball, Miss Sheely?''

''All this to avoid the terror of a blind date.'' She laughed without mirth. ''You really are desperate.''

''Yes.'' He lifted her hand to his lips. ''I am desperate, Callie. I'm desperate to make things right between us. I'm desperate to chuck our stupid agreement about keeping our relationship strictly professional.''

She stared at him. ''But you said—''

''If I was the one who said it, I was an idiot. If you were the one, would you give me a chance to change your mind? Because I want both, I want it all. My professional relationship with Nurse Sheely and my personal relationship with Callie. I love you, Callie Sheely.''

She looked at him with her heart in her eyes. "I love you, too, Trey Weldon."

It seemed to be the most natural thing in the world for him to reach for her and for her to come slowly into his arms. His mouth moved on hers with a warm, lazy pressure, parting her lips with his tongue as the kiss grew deeper and more intimate.

He felt her passion ignite from the fires of his own as she slid her arms around his neck and melted against him. He moved his hand over her cotton T-shirt, cupping her breast.

Callie moaned and arched against his palm, slipping her jeans-clad leg over him. Trey needed no more encouragement. He stood up and carried her into her bedroom.

This time they undressed each other slowly, pausing to kiss and caress as each item of clothing was discarded. This time they were not in the dark. Callie's small ceramic lamp was lit on the nightstand.

Between kisses, they feasted on the sight of each other's bodies as they hadn't been able to do before.

"You're so beautiful," Trey sighed, as he watched his thumb circle the dusky tips of her milky-white breasts. "I knew you would be. And now I'm finally able to see you..." He sighed with pleasure, gently taking her nipple between his lips.

It was Callie's turn to breathe a sigh. She moved her hands over his strong, muscular body, savoring the contrasting textures of his smooth skin and the wiry mat of hair covering certain areas. She explored every intriguing erogenous zone, and when her fingers finally closed around him, she smiled at his gasp.

"There is something in the drawer of the nightstand," she said, straightening to reach inside it. "Something to ease your mind about any little consequences."

She removed a small box of condoms. "I bought these today."

"After refusing to go to the ball with me, after your declaration that we could only have a professional relationship with no more thrills and passion?'' He gave her a mock-stern glare but couldn't keep up even that teasing pretense. He grinned sheepishly at her. ''We must've been operating on the same wavelength because in my jacket is the same thing, right down to the exact brand. How did you know which ones to buy?''

''I just grabbed the first box I saw.'' Callie tore open the foil packet. ''Mrs. Radocay would say we were psychically attuned, but truly, I think it's the result of good product placement.''

''I like Mrs. Radocay's version better. It's more romantic than your marketing theory. Should I help you with that?'' He watched her reach for him, his blue eyes hot with passion.

''I think I can manage, Dr. Weldon.''

And she did, very well. The deft coordination which made her a superb operating room nurse served them both very well in the bedroom, too.

Trey filled her with a powerful thrust, and she cried out his name, clinging to him, thrilling to the sublime pleasure of their merged bodies. Their eyes locked, and the intensity of their gaze was fierce. Looking into each other's eyes as they made love was like a baring of souls.

They didn't speak; they communicated their feelings with their bodies rather than words. They moved together in rapturous rhythm, until both gave up control and allowed the passionate blaze to consume them in a conflagration of ecstasy....

Afterward, Callie and Trey lay together for a long time, kissing, their naked bodies pressed against each other, her softness to his hardness, their hands and fingers leisurely stroking and caressing.

''You know, you never did get around to accepting my invitation to the Springtime Ball,'' Trey said much later, after they had showered together and were back in bed holding each other. "Dare I assume that you've reconsidered my offer and the answer is yes?"

"I think you can safely assume that," she teased, playfully nibbling on his sensual lower lip. "Yes, my answer is yes. If…you think your parents won't mind me as your date."

"Why would they mind? My mother is thrilled with the idea of me having a *girlfriend*." He chuckled at the word. "You'll like my parents, Callie. They aren't snobs. They—" He took a deep breath, suddenly turning serious. "There is no way they could be. Callie, I have something to tell you."

She raised herself up on one elbow and stared at him. "What is it, Trey?"

"This isn't a deep, dark secret but it's something I don't tell people. Only the ones who knew at the time know. Does that make sense?"

"A little. Tell me, Trey."

"I wasn't born a Weldon," he blurted, as if rushing the words out would make it more tolerable to say.

Callie studied him, observing his tension, perceiving the sadness underlying it. "Were you adopted?" she asked quietly.

It certainly made no difference to her, but she could tell it mattered a great deal to Trey. She remained silent, stroking her fingers along his back, waiting for him to continue when he was ready.

"Half." He laughed slightly at her bewildered look. "I am my mother's biological son. She married Winston Weldon when I was four, and he adopted me immediately after. The day I officially became his son was one of the happiest days of my life. And yes, I remember it very well, though I was only four. Win Jr., who was fourteen at the time, carried me on his shoulders into the dining room of the house where there was an elaborate cake and told me how glad he was to have a little brother."

"He sounds nice, Trey," Callie said softly. And not at all like the snobby stuffed shirt she'd imagined.

"He's the best brother anyone could have, and Dad is the best father!" Trey's face glowed as he talked about them. Callie was touched. "I wanted to be exactly like them, I have always been determined to make them proud of me. I would've gladly gone into their investment firm with them, but I had this aptitude for science and was fascinated with neurological research and surgery. The family encouraged me to go where my talents lay. They've always been supportive. They are everything a family could ever be."

"They must be tremendously proud of you, Trey. You're everything a son could ever be," Callie said loyally. She sensed he was holding something back. That his family story, which had such happy results, was not quite complete.

"What about your birth father?" she asked, intuiting that might be the missing chapter. "He would've had to sign away his parental rights for Mr. Weldon to adopt you, right?"

"He wasn't around, thank God!" Trey's expression grew hard. "He was a worthless excuse for a human being, a bully, a criminal, in and out of jail since his teens. My mother met him back in the sixties when he was playing the part of a counterculture rebel and she was a nice middle-class kid who was bored and spoiled and tired of being a good girl. The best thing he did for her was to make her his widow. It sounds harsh, but it's the truth."

"Uh-oh." Callie frowned, thinking of the books and movies about those times and those characters. There usually wasn't a happy ending for the mismatched couple. Obviously, things hadn't worked out between Trey's natural parents, either.

"Mom got pregnant with my sister Trina and later with me. Her family disowned her, and she was stuck with two little kids and *him,* who by then had shown his true colors. He was a sociopath, not a hippie. He drank, he stole, he beat my mother and sister and me. My mother doesn't think I have any memories of any of this because I wasn't quite three when he was killed. But I remember. I remember *him*. He's been a cautionary figure to me all my life, embodying what I never wanted to be. Just carrying his genes makes me uneasy.''

''Which is why you were so disturbed about all that genetic speculation about the Hagen boy,'' Callie concluded, understanding now. Understanding so much more about him than she had before. ''Trey, there is no genetic curse. People make their own choices. You've chosen well and always will. Don't be haunted by your dead ex-father,'' she pleaded earnestly.

''My dead ex-father.'' Trey managed a smile. ''Well, I've been very fortunate in my adoptive father, haven't I?''

''What about your sister?'' Callie swallowed, guessing the answer. There had never been mention of a sister, not in the newspaper article, not by Trey himself, until now.

''She was killed in a car accident shortly after she'd turned five.''

''Trey, I'm so sorry.'' Callie held him tight, trying to absorb some of the grief and anger that still lingered within him.

''Trina was with *him*, who else?'' Trey's voice was bitter. ''He was out on parole and had just robbed—what else?— a liquor store. Then he took off. He was estimated to be speeding over a hundred miles an hour, so it didn't take long for a patrol car to spot him. He shot at the police during the chase, and it ended with his car wrapped around a pole. He was dead and so was my sister.''

''Poor little girl,'' whispered Callie.

''Losing Trina snapped my mother out of her downward spiral,'' Trey continued. ''She reconciled with her parents, went to work as a receptionist in the Weldon investment firm and enrolled in college night classes. She met Winston, Sr., at the firm. He was a widower. His wife had died of ovarian cancer five years earlier. There was a considerable age difference between Mother and Dad, and I've been told there was plenty of gossip at the time, but that didn't stop them.''

"And it turned out to be true love that lasted." Callie sighed happily.

Her dread of meeting the upper-class Weldons evaporated. Trey was right: they couldn't be snobs, having faced and overcome so many differences. Suddenly it was all so clear to her. She'd been a snob, a reverse snob, building imaginary barriers based on her *own* stereotype of the upper class. Trey and his family deserved better.

Callie firmly cast aside the doubts and fears. She should've had more sense of her own self-worth, she silently chided herself. After all, Trey valued her; he had proven so by choosing her. *Twice!* First professionally, now personally.

"I can't wait for the Springtime Ball!" she exclaimed, giving him an exuberant hug.

It was all Trey could do to stop himself from proposing to her right then and there. But he didn't. He wanted to do this right, in true Weldon fashion—which did not mean waiting until his fortieth birthday, he realized rather sheepishly. Not when he'd found the woman who was everything he wanted in a wife when he was a mere youth of thirty-three!

Trey smiled with sheer happiness. A proposal in true Weldon fashion definitely required a romantic setting…like the Springtime Ball?

Epilogue

The Annual Tri-State Hospital Springtime Ball was held in the grand ballroom of the downtown William Penn Hotel. The guests danced to music provided by the Purcell Orchestra, and the buffet, featuring a wide assortment of Caribbean fare, was constantly replenished. The decor included strings of colored lanterns and tall papier-mâché palm trees that seemed to sway as if a tropical breeze was blowing.

"I guess this is supposed to be springtime on a Caribbean island because it looks nothing like a Pittsburgh spring," Trey remarked to Callie as he led her onto the dance floor.

"They try to have different motifs every year," said Callie. "Although the time they tried to have an arctic decor there were a lot of jokes."

"I wonder why?" Trey murmured drolly. "Spring is supposed to be beautiful in the arctic circle. So different from the other seasons there." He pulled her into his arms.

They moved to the music in perfect sync, their steps matching, as if they'd been dancing together for years.

"You dance as well as you do everything else, Dr. Weldon," said Callie, laughing up into his eyes. "You might not have liked Miss Martha's dancing lessons, but she taught you well. Of course, since you are so amazingly well coordinated, it would be impossible for you to have two left feet."

He caught her reference to the conversation with the ingratiating med student and smiled. "I never liked dancing because I considered it a waste of my valuable time. But having you as my partner changes everything." He bent his head and lightly kissed her forehead. "You look beautiful tonight, Callie."

She felt beautiful. Her new silk dress was a vibrant rainbow of colors with a waist-cinching sash. It cost more than she'd ever spent on any dress but Callie didn't regret spending a single penny. Sometimes impulse buying could be fun. Her hair swung thick and bouncy and full around her shoulders.

"I like your parents, Trey," she told him, and they both glanced over at the table where Winston Weldon, Sr., was rising from his chair to lead his wife onto the dance floor.

Trey had his mother's dark hair and blue eyes, but she was petite and small-boned. It seemed that Trey had inherited his height and his big, strong frame from his biological father. But that was all. In every way Trey was the antithesis of that man.

"My folks like you, too," Trey assured her, following her gaze to see his parents dancing.

Callie smiled. She'd hit it off immediately with Win and Laura Weldon when she'd met them at the cocktail party that the Weldons' friends had hosted before the ball. They were funny and pleasant and easy to talk to. Nothing at all like the stiff snobs she'd once feared.

"We've spent time with my parents and their friends tonight, we've hung with the OR crowd, can we spend a little time alone now?" Trey asked, sounding plaintive.

"Would you like to find a utility closet to duck into?"

"Don't tempt me." He shot her a smoldering look. "Come with me."

She could almost feel the excitement emanating from him as he led her out onto the terrace. It was chilly outside but not unbearably cold, and at least it wasn't raining. The music sounded muted but lent a romantic air.

Callie looked up into Trey's glittering blue eyes.

"I wanted to do this inside, preferably your apartment, where it's warm and there is a bed available, but my mother convinced me that I needed a unique romantic setting to make this memorable." He reached inside the pocket of his tuxedo jacket and brought out a small velvet box.

The kind that a ring came in. Callie felt her heart lurch crazily. Whatever the setting, she had a feeling this was going to be one of the most memorable moments of her life.

"I love you, Callie," Trey said, his eyes, his voice filled with emotion. "You're everything I've always wanted in a woman. Until I met you, I didn't know what was missing in my life."

He removed a beautiful diamond ring. "I'd get down on one knee, but the ground is still damp from this morning's rain," he murmured wryly. Then he took her hand in his. "Callie, will you marry me?"

Tears welled in her eyes. She didn't know it was possible to be this happy, that dreams really did come true. "I love you, Trey." She threw her arms around him. "I love you so much."

"Then let me put this ring on your finger and say yes."

"Yes!"

He slipped the ring on her finger and they kissed. A slow, deep and tender kiss.

"I guess this is the beginning of a long engagement," Callie said when they finally surfaced to breathe. "Seven years till you're forty, hmm?"

"I should've expected you to throw that one at me." Trey

was grinning, looking as happy as she was. "I did this the traditional way and called your dad to ask for your hand in marriage. He was very glad to hear that I wasn't gay. As of yesterday he'd already sent in his deposit to the place for our wedding reception. According to your mom, our wedding date is the week before Christmas. I guess I should ask if that's all right with you?"

"It's perfect, Trey."

*   *   *   *   *

FORTUNE'S Children™

The Fortune family requests
your presence at the weddings of

Silhouette Desire's provocative new miniseries
featuring the beloved Fortune family and
five of your favorite authors.

Bride of Fortune—August 2000
by Leanne Banks (SD #1311)

Mail-Order Cinderella—September 2000
by Kathryn Jensen (SD #1318)

Fortune's Secret Child—October 2000
by Shawna Delacorte (SD #1324)

Husband—or Enemy?—November 2000
by Caroline Cross (SD #1330)

Groom of Fortune—December 2000
by Peggy Moreland (SD #1336)

Don't miss these unforgettable romances...
available at your favorite retail outlet.

Where love comes alive™

If you enjoyed what you just read,
then we've got an offer you can't resist!

Take 2 bestselling love stories FREE!

Plus get a FREE surprise gift!

Look Who's Celebrating Our 20th Anniversary:

Celebrate 20 YEARS

"Twenty years of Silhouette! I can hardly believe it. Looking back on it, I find that my life and my books for Silhouette were inextricably intertwined.... Every Silhouette I wrote was a piece of my life. So, thank you, Silhouette, and may you have many more anniversaries."

—International bestselling author
Candace Camp

"I wish you continued success, Silhouette Books.... Thank you for giving me a chance to do what I love best in all the world."

—International bestselling author
Diana Palmer

"For twenty years Silhouette has thrilled us with love stories that ring true in the hearts and souls of millions of readers who know that happy endings are truly women's noblest goals. Way to go, Silhouette!"

—International bestselling author
Ann Major

Silhouette
Desire

COMING NEXT MONTH

#1309 THE RETURN OF ADAMS CADE—BJ James
Man of the Month/Men of Belle Terre

An outcast from his home, Adams Cade had returned to Belle Terre to face his family—and his childhood love, Eden Claibourne. But when their reunion was threatened by Adams' past, could Eden convince him that his true home was in her arms?

#1310 TALLCHIEF: THE HOMECOMING—Cait London
Body & Soul/The Tallchiefs

The discovery of Liam Tallchief's heritage was still raw when sassy Michelle Farrell barreled into his life doing her best to unravel all his secrets. Michelle had never been a woman to stay in one place too long. So when Liam kissed her, why did she feel a fierce urge to claim *him?*

#1311 BRIDE OF FORTUNE—Leanne Banks
Fortune's Children: The Grooms

Accustomed to working with powerful men, Adele O'Neil instinctively knew that it would take a brave woman to get close to larger-than-life Jason Fortune. Could she be that woman? His touch must have jumbled her brain, because she was suddenly dreaming of home and hearth....

#1312 THE LAST SANTINI VIRGIN—Maureen Child
Bachelor Battalion

When Gunnery Sergeant Nick Paretti was ordered by his major to take dance lessons, he never expected his partner to be feisty virgin Gina Santini. And though the sparks flew when they were pressed cheek to cheek, Gina yearned for so much more. Could this gruff marine become Gina's partner—in marriage?

#1313 IN NAME ONLY—Peggy Moreland
Texas Grooms

Preacher's daughter Shelby Cannon needed a father for her unborn child—and rodeo cowboy Troy Jacobs was the perfect candidate. Only problem was, the two would have to be married in-name-only...and Troy was determined to make his temporary bride into his forever wife!

#1314 ONE SNOWBOUND WEEKEND...—Christy Lockhart
There was a snowstorm outside, a warm fire in his house, and Shane Masters's ex-wife was in front of him declaring her love. Shane knew that Angie had amnesia, but as they were trapped together for the weekend, he had only one choice—to invite her in and this time never let her go....

CMN0700